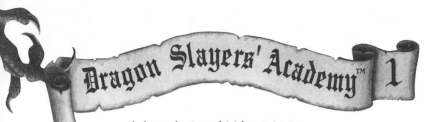

THE NEW KID
AT SCHOOL

Dragon Slayers' Academy™ 1

THE NEW KID
AT SCHOOL

By K.H. McMullan
Illustrated by Bill Basso

GROSSET & DUNLAP • NEW YORK

For Mrs. Roché-Albert
and all the great kids
in her class at P.S. 116
—K.H. McM.

Text copyright © 1997 by K.H. McMullan. Illustrations copyright © 1997 by Bill Basso.
All rights reserved. Published by Grosset & Dunlap, a division of Penguin Putnam Books
for Young Readers, New York. DRAGON SLAYERS' ACADEMY is a trademark of The
Putnam & Grosset Group. GROSSET & DUNLAP is a trademark of Grosset & Dunlap,
Inc. Published simultaneously in Canada. Printed in the U.S.A.

Library of Congress Cataloging-in-Publication Data
McMullan, K.H.
  The new kid at school / by K.H. McMullan ; illustrated by Bill Basso.
    p. cm. — (Dragon Slayers' Academy ; 1)
  Summary: Wiglaf is off to Dragon Slayers' Academy and in for a first day of school he
will never forget.
  [1. Dragons—Fiction. 2. First day of school—Fiction. 3. Schools—Fiction.]
  I. Basso, Bill, ill. II. Title. III. Series: McMullan, K.H. Dragon Slayers' Academy; 1.
PZ7.M47879Ne 1997   97-15520
  [E] — dc21   CIP
                                                                                                                        AC

ISBN 0-448-42289-1   A B C E F G H I J

Chapter 1

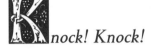*nock! Knock!*

"Who's there?" Fergus bellowed from inside the hovel.

"A poor minstrel!" came a voice from out in the blizzard.

"A poor minstrel who?" Fergus called.

"Please! I am freezing!" cried the minstrel. "This is no time for a joke!"

"Pity!" Fergus yelled. "There's nothing I like better than a good knock-knock!"

He yanked open the door. There stood a snow-covered man with a lute and a pack slung over his shoulder. Icicles hung from his nose and ears. His lips were blue from the cold.

"Be gone, varlet!" Fergus shouted through his dirty yellow beard. "There is no room here!"

Fergus spoke the truth. His whole hovel was but one cramped room, which he shared with his wife, Molwena, and their thirteen sons.

Twelve of these sons were big, beefy lads with greasy yellow hair like their father's. They scowled out the door at the minstrel, shouting, "Be gone! Be gone!"

But the third-eldest son, Wiglaf, was different from his brothers. He was small for his age. He had hair the color of carrots. And he could not bear to see any creature suffer.

When Fergus reached out to slam the door in the shivering minstrel's face, Wiglaf grabbed his arm.

"Wait, Father!" he said. "Could not the minstrel sleep in the pigsty?"

"I sing songs and tell fortunes," the minstrel offered.

"Songs? Fortunes?" Fergus growled. "Pig droppings!"

"I also chop wood, shovel snow, slop pigs, rake dung, scrub floors, and wash dishes," the minstrel added quickly.

"Oh, but we have Wiglaf to do all that," Molwena told him.

"Please!" the minstrel begged through his chattering teeth. "There must be *something* I can do in return for a roof over my head."

Fergus scratched his beard and tried to think.

"He might kill rats for us, Fergus," Molwena suggested. "Wiglaf won't do that."

"Wiglaf feels sorry for the rats," one of the younger brothers told the minstrel.

"Wiglaf won't squish a cockroach," another

brother tattled. "He won't even swat a fly."

"Wiggie never wants to kill anything," complained a third. "I was pulling the legs off a spider once, and—"

"I have it!" Fergus bellowed suddenly. "The minstrel can kill rats to earn his keep!" He grinned. "Show him to the sty, Wiglaf!"

So Wiglaf did just that. And later on he took a bowl of Molwena's cabbage soup out to the minstrel for his supper.

"Ah! Hot soup to warm my cold bones!" The minstrel took a sip. "Gaaach!" he cried, and spat it out.

"It is foul-tasting at first," Wiglaf admitted. "But you'll get used to it."

"I must or I shall starve," the minstrel said. "Talk to me, lad, while I try to get it down." Then he held his nose and jammed a spoonful into his mouth.

"You are lucky to bed out here with the pigs," Wiglaf told him. "The sty smells far better than our hovel, for my father believes that bathing causes madness. And Daisy, here"—he patted the head of a plump young pig sitting next to him—"she is my best friend. And far better company than my brothers. They only like to fight and bloody each other's noses."

Wiglaf rubbed his own nose. It was still tender from one of his brother's fists.

"They gang up on me something awful," he added. "Then they call me a blister and a runt because I will not fight back. I know it is foolish," he went on, "but sometimes I dream that one day I will become a mighty hero. Would not *that* surprise my brothers!"

"No doubt it would," the minstrel said. He jammed one last spoonful of soup into his mouth. Then he burped. "Ah! That's better. Now, my boy, I know some tales of mighty heroes. Would you care to hear one?"

"I would, indeed!" Wiglaf exclaimed.

No one had ever told Wiglaf a tale before. Oh, Molwena sometimes told him what she would do to him if he did not wash the dishes. And Fergus often told him how he was no use at all in the cabbage fields. But those tales were not so much fun to hear.

Wiglaf settled down in the straw next to his pig to listen. The tale was indeed about a mighty hero. A hero who tried to slay a dragon named Gorzil.

When at last the minstrel came to the end, his voice dropped low. "Then Gorzil roared a roar of thunder. Bolts of lightning shot from his nose. And from out of the fire and smoke came a CRUNCH...CRUNCH...CRUNCH! And a mighty GULP!

"When the smoke cleared, the knight and his steed were gone," the minstrel said. "But Gorzil was sitting high on his pile of gold—using the knight's own sword for a toothpick."

"No!" cried Wiglaf.

"'Tis true," the minstrel told the boy. "My grandfather was a dragon hunter. He saw it happen with his own two eyes—well, with his one good eye, anyway."

"Pray, tell," Wiglaf asked, "who finally killed this dragon?"

"Oh, Gorzil is still very much alive." The minstrel grew thoughtful. "My grandfather told me that every dragon has a secret weakness. Take Old Snart, for instance. For years, that dragon set fire to villages for sport. Then one day Sir Gilford stuck out his tongue and said, 'Nonny-nonny poo-poo, you old sissy!' Well, Old Snart hated to be teased. He began whimpering and crying until he collapsed in a pool of tears. He hardly noticed when Sir Gilford sliced off his head."

"And what is the dragon Gorzil's weakness?" Wiglaf asked.

"That," said the minstrel, "no one knows." He picked up his lute. "I have written a song about Gorzil. Listen:

"Gorzil is a dragon, a greedy one is he,
From his jaws of terror, villagers do flee.
Gorzil burps up clouds of smoke,
Shoots lightning from his snout....
Where, oh, where's the hero
Who'll find his secret out?"

From that night on, Wiglaf brought the minstrel a bowl of cabbage soup for supper. In return, the minstrel told Wiglaf many a dragon tale. And he taught the boy many a useful skill: how to stand on his head; how to wiggle his ears; and how to imitate the call of a lovesick toad.

By the time the snow began to melt, he had even taught the boy how to read and write.

Then one spring morning, Wiglaf brought the pigs their slop and found the minstrel packing.

"Are you off for good?" Wiglaf asked sadly.

"Aye, lad. A minstrel must wander," the minstrel explained. "And"—he burped—"eat something besides cabbage soup. But here, give me your hand. Before I go, I shall tell your fortune."

Wiglaf held out his palm. The minstrel studied it for a long time.

"What do you see?" Wiglaf finally asked.

"Something I never thought to see," the minstrel replied. "The lines on your palm say that you were born to be a mighty hero!"

"Me?" Wiglaf cried. "Are you sure?"

The minstrel nodded. "In all my years of telling fortunes, I have never been wrong."

"Imagine!" Wiglaf exclaimed. "But what brave deed will I do?"

"That," said the minstrel, "you must discover for yourself. Now I must be off. I shall miss you, Wiglaf."

"Wait!" Wiglaf said. He reached into his tunic and pulled out a tattered piece of cloth. "This is all I have left of...well, of something I had when I was very young. I carry it with me always, for good luck." He held the rag out to the minstrel. "Here. I should like you to have it."

"Keep your good-luck charm, Wiglaf," the minstrel said, shouldering his lute. "The road a hero travels is never an easy one. I fear you shall need much luck."

And with that he was gone.

Chapter 2

"Knock! Knock!" Fergus bellowed one fine summer morning at the breakfast table.

Wiglaf didn't answer. He poked at his cabbage pancake, lost in his own thoughts.

It had been months since the minstrel went away. And as far as Wiglaf could tell, he had not become a hero. True, he had saved a chipmunk from drowning in the pigs' water trough. And he had rescued six spiders from his brothers' cruel hands. But surely these were not the deeds of a mighty hero.

Wiglaf kept brooding. He never noticed Fergus bending down close to his ear.

"KNOCK! KNOCK!" Fergus shouted.

Wiglaf jumped. "Who—who's there?"

"Harry!" Fergus cried.

"Harry who?" asked Wiglaf.

"Harry up and eat your pancakes!" Fergus roared. "We go to the Pinwick Fair today!"

"Hooray!" yelled one of Wiglaf's little brothers. "Jugglers and lepers! Let us be off!"

"And so we shall be," Molwena promised, "as soon as Wiglaf does the dishes."

"We could be off sooner if someone dried," Wiglaf hinted.

"Nah," said the eldest brother. "We'll wait."

And so Wiglaf scrubbed the dishes. Then he dried them. Then he put them away.

At last the family set off for the village.

Just outside Pinwick, Fergus stopped beside the village message tree. He squinted at a new notice tacked to its trunk.

"Wiglaf!" Fergus shouted. "The minstrel showed you how to make sense of these squiggles. Tell us what this sign says!"

Wiglaf stepped up and read: "Dragon Slayers' Academy."

Fergus frowned. "Acada...*what?*"

"Academy," Wiglaf repeated. "It means school."

"I know *that*," his father said. "Go on."

"We teach our students to slay dragons," Wiglaf read.

Slay dragons? Wiglaf thought with growing interest. *Heroes slayed dragons!*

"And," he read on, "they bring the dragons' hoards home to *you!*"

"The dragons' hoards?" Fergus scratched his armpit thoughtfully. "That would be... what?"

"Gold and jewels, most likely," Wiglaf replied.

"Blazing King Ken's britches!" Fergus roared. "Read it all!" Which is just what Wiglaf was dying to do:

Is there a lazy lad hanging about your hovel? Is he eating more than his share of your good cabbage soup? Don't you wish he could earn his keep?

"I'll say," snorted Molwena.

Dragon Slayers' Academy is your answer! Feast your eyes on just a few of our classes:

- *How to Stalk a Fire-Breather*
- *How to Get Close to a Dragon*
- *How to Get Even Closer*
- *How to Get Really, Really Close*
- *101 Ways to Slay*

Best of all, we will teach your boy how to bring a dragon's golden hoard home to you!

Just look at what some of our fine lads have done:

Baldrick the Bold
Baldrick slew three dragons! With their golden hoards, he bought his lucky parents a 450-room castle!

"That would do for us," Molwena muttered.

Torblad the Terrible
Two kills. Two hoards. Now his mum and pop just lie about and watch other folk work.

"Oh, boy!" said Fergus.

Angus the Avenger
Angus slew a whole nest of dragon young! His parents now dress in nothing but silk and velvet.

"Do they, now?!" Molwena exclaimed. "I wonder how much this school costs."

The fee? Only 7 pennies! (Plus a teensy part of each hoard.) Send us your sons! We turn useless lads into HEROES who go for the gold!

Signed,
Mordred the Marvelous, Headmaster, DSA (Located just off Huntsman's Path, east of the Dark Forest)

Dragon slaying, thought Wiglaf. It sounded pretty gruesome. But dragons were evil. They deserved to be slain—didn't they? And who slew them? Mighty heroes, that's who!

Maps tacked to the tree showed the way from Pinwick to Dragon Slayers' Academy. Wiglaf pulled one off and stared at it. Here was a path he might follow to become a hero!

"Father?" Wiglaf began eagerly, "I would—"

"Quiet!" Fergus barked. He turned to his eldest son. "Do you want to go to the acad... to the school?" he asked him.

The eldest picked at a scab on his ear. "Would I get in trouble for fighting and knocking other boys' teeth out?" he asked.

Fergus nodded. "You might."

"I wouldn't like that," the eldest declared.

Wiglaf tried again. "Father, I—"

"Shush!" Fergus turned to his second-eldest. "Do you want to go to the school?" he asked him.

The second-eldest scratched a bedbug bite on his neck. "Would I have to comb my hair and change my britches?" he asked.

Fergus nodded again. "Most likely."

"Then I won't go," the second-eldest said.

"I will, Father!" Wiglaf exclaimed. "Pray, send me!"

But Fergus only rolled his eyes and turned to his fourth-eldest. "You're a big, strapping lad," he began. "How would you—"

"Wait, Father!" Wiglaf cut in. "Think on this: If I slay a dragon, I shall bring you a mountain of gold! You would like that, would you not?"

"Yes...." Fergus nodded slowly.

"And if the dragon gets the better of me?" Wiglaf went on. "Well, you say I am no use to you in the cabbage fields anyway."

"Hmm...." Fergus tugged at a chicken bone that had been tangled in his beard all week. "I have it!" he roared at last. "I shall send *Wiglaf* to the dragon school! He is no use to me in the cabbage fields anyway!"

"That's a fine idea, Fergus," Molwena put in. "But what about the seven pennies? Where would we get that kind of money?"

Fergus shrugged. "That pig of his should bring seven pennies."

"You mean, sell Daisy?" Wiglaf cried.

Wiglaf's younger brother wiped his nose on

his sleeve. "Daddy?" he said. "When Wiglaf goes, can I have his goatskin to sleep under?"

"Yes, all right," replied their father.

"But—" Wiglaf began.

"Can I have his spoon, then?" asked his even younger brother.

"Yes, yes," answered Fergus.

"Can I have his boots?" asked his still younger brother. "And his britches and his tunic?"

"Wait!" Wiglaf cried. "I'm not dead, am I? I still need my clothes! And I shall never sell Daisy! Never!"

"Oh, do be quiet," Molwena scolded. "How else are you going to get seven pennies?"

Wiglaf folded his arms across his chest. "I shall find a way."

"Mommy," one of the younger brothers whined, "I want to go to the fair! I want to see the two-headed calf."

"Of course you do!" Molwena exclaimed.

"And we don't want to miss the hanging." She turned away from the tree, and the rest of the family followed.

All but Wiglaf. He straggled behind, thinking. He was going away to Dragon Slayers' Academy! And, somehow, he was going to keep Daisy by his side.

Wiglaf smiled. At last he was on his way to becoming a mighty hero.

Chapter 3

"Well, farewell!" Wiglaf said the next morning at dawn. Fergus and Molwena and a few of his brothers had gotten up to see him off.

Fergus slapped Wiglaf on the back and roared, "Knock! Knock!"

"Who's there?" called a little brother.

"Oliver!" said Fergus.

"Oliver who?" asked another little brother.

"Oliver troubles will be over when Wiglaf comes home with the gold!" Fergus cried. He slapped him on the back again.

"Off you go," Molwena said. "Get a good price for the pig."

"And don't come home without the gold!" Fergus added.

Wiglaf picked up his pack. Inside were six cabbage dumplings, a loaf of cabbage bread, and a pickled cabbage tart. He had also put in a length of rope, the map, and his lucky rag.

"Ready, Daisy?" Wiglaf asked.

The faithful pig glanced up at him and wagged her curly tail. Then the two of them set off for Dragon Slayers' Academy.

They walked south all morning. Around noon, they came to Nowhere Swamp. The minstrel had told Wiglaf tales of this spot. Hungry serpents lurked in the slimy water. Hungry vultures circled overhead. Mad hermits lived in every cave and hollow tree. And most of them were hungry, too.

But worst of all was the quicksand. It was so quick it could suck a boy down—*slurp!*—before he could cry for help. A traveler had to be very careful to get across it with his life.

Wiglaf studied his map closely. "We must cross here, Daisy," he said. "I shall carry you."

Wiglaf picked up the pig and started along the spine of rocks jutting out from the quicksand. Wiglaf knew that one false step and—*slurp!*—he would never be a hero.

On a big, flat rock halfway across, Wiglaf stopped. He put Daisy down and searched the swamp to see how far they still had to go.

"Daisy!" Wiglaf cried. "A pointed hat is sinking in the quicksand! And look! There is a *head* beneath the hat!"

Daisy squealed in alarm.

Wiglaf cupped his hands to his mouth. "Stay where you are!" he shouted to the head. "I shall save you!"

Wiglaf grabbed the rope from his pack. His heart thumped. He never thought that he would be a hero *this* soon! But before he could throw the rope, the hat and head started to rise.

Wiglaf watched, amazed, as a man with a long white beard floated up, out of the sand. He wore a wide-sleeved blue robe dotted with silver stars. He glided over the quicksand toward Wiglaf and Daisy.

Now Daisy squealed in fright.

The man came to a stop in front of Wiglaf. "Don't you have anything better to do than annoy me?" he grumbled. "And turn off that pig!"

Instantly, Daisy stopped squealing.

"I am sorry," Wiglaf managed. "Are—are you a wizard?"

"No, I'm a fairy princess!" the man snapped. "Of course I'm a wizard. You know anyone else who wears a long blue robe with stars on it? I don't think so. Zelnoc's the name," he went on. "And your name is...wait." The wizard squeezed his eyes shut. "Don't tell me. It's coming. Ah! I have it. Wigwam! No...Waglump!"

"Close," Wiglaf said. "I am Wiglaf. And this is my pig, Daisy."

"Charmed." The wizard gave a little wave. "Now, Wuglop, what was all that yelling about? And what's with the rope?"

"I was going to rescue you from the quicksand," Wiglaf explained.

Zelnoc shook his head. "Do you know nothing of wizards, my boy? I wasn't sinking. I was in for repairs. This part of the swamp is known as Wizard's Bog. The quicksand here has strong powers. You see, sometimes my spells go wrong...." He shrugged. "It's not your problem. So tell me. What are you doing out here in the middle of Nowhere?"

"I am on my way to Dragon Slayers' Academy," Wiglaf said proudly.

"You're kidding!" Zelnoc exclaimed. "*You* are a dragon slayer?"

"Not yet," Wiglaf admitted. "But a minstrel told my fortune. He said that I was born to be a hero. And heroes slay dragons, do they not?"

"Some do, I suppose," the wizard said. "Well, I wish you luck, Wicklamp. And speaking of wishes, what'll it be?"

"I beg your pardon?" Wiglaf said.

"Your wish!" Zelnoc repeated. "You *did* interrupt me, it's true. But you meant well. And Wizard Rule Number 364 says every good deed must be rewarded. So wish away, Wigloop. But make it snappy. I haven't got all day."

"All right," Wiglaf agreed. "I wish for... seven pennies!"

Zelnoc shook his head. "Sorry, kid. Wizards never carry cash."

"I see." Wiglaf thought for a moment. Then he said, "How about a suit of armor?"

"No, no, no," the wizard scolded. "Only *knights* wear armor!"

Wiglaf sighed. "What should I wish for?"

"A sword," Zelnoc told him.

"All right," said Wiglaf. "I wish for a sword."

"An excellent choice!" exclaimed the wizard. "And have I got a sword for you!"

Zelnoc reached up his left sleeve and pulled out a stumpy metal blade. It was badly bent, dented, and covered with rust.

"This is Surekill," Zelnoc said. "It was made for dragon slaying. It has great power."

"Oh, is it a magic sword?" Wiglaf asked hopefully.

"Would I give you any other kind?" Zelnoc rolled his eyes. "Now, here's what you do. Point Surekill at your enemy and say..." The wizard frowned. "What is it, now? 'Surekill, go get 'em!'? No... 'Surekill, do your thing!'? No. But it's something like that. Anyway, when you do get it right, Surekill will leap from your hand and obey."

"Uh...thank you," Wiglaf said, taking the weapon and tucking it into his belt. He supposed a rusty, dented sword was better than no sword at all.

Zelnoc glanced at Daisy. "What about the pig?" he asked. "Does she have a wish?"

"If only she could talk, she might tell you," Wiglaf answered.

"Talk?" Zelnoc's eyes lit up. "I have just the thing! My speech spell!"

The wizard pushed up his sleeves, stretched his hands toward Daisy, and began to chant: "Oink-a-la, doink-a-la, fee fi fig! This pig shall be a talking pig!"

Daisy blinked, and very softly she said, "Iglaf-way?"

"She speaks!" Wiglaf cried. "Yet in what strange tongue?"

"Maybe Greek?" the wizard guessed.

"E-may, alking-tay!" Daisy burbled happily.

"I know!" Wiglaf exclaimed. "'Tis Pig Latin!"

"Excuse me?" Zelnoc said.

"Pig Latin," Wiglaf said. "You know—where you take the first sound in a word and put it at the end. Then you add the 'ay' sound. Pig becomes 'ig-pay.' Do you see?"

"Pig Latin, my foot!" Zelnoc moaned. "My spell went wrong!"

"O-nay idding-kay!" Daisy scoffed.

"Stop, pig!" Zelnoc cried. "That crazy language makes my beard twitch." He shuddered. "I'm in worse shape than I thought. And the Wizards' Convention is only two weeks away.

Zelnoc turned and began gliding back to the center of the bog.

"Good-bye, Waglap!" he called. "Good luck with the dragons!"

"Good-bye!" Wiglaf called back.

"O-say ong-lay!" Daisy squealed.

Then, with a loud *slurp*, the quicksand swallowed up the wizard, this time hat and all.

Chapter 4

iglaf checked his map by the light of the full moon. Yes, this had to be the place—Dragon Slayers' Academy.

"In truth, this is not what I expected," Wiglaf muttered.

"Uck-yay," Daisy agreed.

Wiglaf and Daisy stood at the edge of a moat filled with greenish, foul-smelling water. It reminded Wiglaf, in many ways, of Molwena's cabbage soup.

A rickety drawbridge led over the water to a gatehouse set in the middle of the broken-down castle wall. A tattered blue banner waved above the door. Bold letters on it spelled out DSA.

Wiglaf drew a deep breath and started across the drawbridge. Daisy trotted at his side.

Wiglaf pulled a chain by the gatehouse door. A bell sounded from deep within.

After a time, the door cracked open. A short man with big eyes stared out at the travelers. He held a torch in one hand.

"Yes?" he said.

"I am Wiglaf, sir," Wiglaf offered. "I am here to study."

"Welcome to DSA!" the man said, opening the door. Wiglaf saw that he wore an apron. "Odd time to arrive, midnight," the man went on. "And school started two weeks ago. But no matter. First things first." He held out his hand. "Seven pennies, please."

"Alas," Wiglaf sighed. "I have no pennies."

The door began to close.

"Wait, sir!" he called. "I—I have half a cabbage dumpling!"

The door banged shut.

"I am a willing worker!" Wiglaf added. "I wash dishes and—"

The door opened a few inches. The man stuck his head out.

"You are skilled at washing dishes?" he asked.

Wiglaf nodded. "Very skilled."

"Well, that suits me better than seven pennies any day." The man opened wide the door. "Come in, come in. I am Frypot, school cook. And former dishwasher."

"Oh, I thank you, kind sir!" Wiglaf exclaimed.

"But say not a word of this to Headmaster Mordred," Frypot warned. "He will put the thumbscrews to me if he finds out."

"Not a word, sir," Wiglaf promised. Then he and Daisy started through the door.

"Hold up now!" Frypot cried. "No pigs allowed!"

"But, sir," Wiglaf began. "This is no ordinary pig! Just listen. Daisy, say hello to the kind man."

"Ello-hay, ypot-Fray!" Daisy said.

"Zounds!" Frypot exclaimed. "A pig that speaks Pig Latin!"

Frypot knelt down next to Daisy.

"Ello-hay, iggy-pay," he said slowly and loudly. "Oh, I shall make you a comfy pallet in the henhouse! Yes, just as soon as I sign in our new dishwasher—er, I mean student."

Then Frypot lit the way through the gatehouse, across the castle yard, and up a stone stairway into the crumbling castle.

Just inside the door, Frypot stuck his torch into a holder on the wall. Then he sat down at a desk and opened a thick book.

"Full name?" he asked.

"Wiglaf of Pinwick."

"Age?"

"This shall be my twelfth summer."

"Skills?"

"Washing dishes," began Wiglaf. "Slopping pigs, raking dung—"

"I meant any skills that might be useful in dragon slaying," Frypot said.

Wiglaf thought for a moment. "Nothing comes to mind," he answered.

"Class I, then." Frypot shut the book. He opened a cupboard and took out a blue tunic and a helmet. White letters on the tunic spelled out DSA. He gave them to Wiglaf. "Your uniform," he said.

"The kitchen's that way," Frypot added, handing Wiglaf the torch. "You can start on the dishes while I settle your pig."

Then the cook led Daisy toward the door. "Ome-cay, iggy-pay," he said, "and tell me how you came by your enchantment. I never cook bacon, you know. Well, hardly ever...."

"What a poor sword!" Wiglaf heard someone exclaim.

He half-opened one eye. He had not had much sleep. Frypot had not told him how very, *very* many dirty dishes there would be.

Now Wiglaf saw two boys in DSA tunics standing at the foot of his cot. One was sandy-haired and plump. The other had straight brown hair and a serious face. He was holding Surekill.

"Have you ever drawn this sword in battle?" the boy asked.

"No," Wiglaf answered.

"Have you sliced off anyone's head with it?"

"Of course not!" Wiglaf exclaimed.

"And I'll wager you have never killed a dragon with it, either."

"No," Wiglaf admitted. "But the sword is called Surekill," he added. "So perhaps I shall. I am called Wiglaf."

"I am Eric." The boy tossed Surekill back onto Wiglaf's cot. "I sleep there." He pointed to the far side of the room.

Wiglaf turned to see one of many lumpy cots just like his own. On the wall above it hung a certificate which read: SIR LANCELOT FAN CLUB. Next to that hung a tapestry. It showed a knight plunging a sword into a dragon. Blood gushed from the dragon's side. *Yuck!* thought Wiglaf.

"I have not yet killed a dragon," Eric was saying. "But soon I shall. Not for the gold, but to rid the world of evil! I want—"

"Pray, save it, Eric," the plump boy cut in.

"Or we shall miss breakfast." He turned to Wiglaf, adding, "Don't worry. We are not all so eager as Eric."

Wiglaf put on his DSA tunic and helmet, and followed his roommates to a huge dining hall.

Boys of all sizes sat at long wooden tables labeled "Class I," "Class II," and "Class III." A big boy was tossing slices of burnt toast through the air. Other boys punched and poked and pinched each other for the honor of catching them.

The sight made Wiglaf feel a little homesick.

Wiglaf got in line and picked up his tray. "What's for breakfast?" he asked Eric.

"Fried eel on toast," Eric replied as he took a heaping plateful.

"*Eel?*" Wiglaf cried.

Eric nodded. "Mordred says eating eel is

part of our training," he explained. "Dragon hunters must learn to live on what can be found near a dragon's lair."

The boys carried their trays to the Class I table. Then Wiglaf watched as Eric scooped up a spoonful of greasy eel and eagerly stuffed it into his mouth.

"Ugh!" Wiglaf groaned. "How do dragon hunters do it?"

The plump boy leaned over toward him. "They don't," he whispered. "Eels live in the castle moat, so they do not cost Mordred a cent. *That* is the real reason we are served eel so often."

"How often?" Wiglaf asked in dismay.

"Too often," the boy replied. "By the way, I am Angus."

Wiglaf stared in awe. "Angus the Avenger?"

"Oh, you saw the notice." Angus smiled shyly. "Mordred only made me sound fierce to attract fierce pupils to his school."

"Then...you never killed a nest of dragon young?" Wiglaf asked.

"Not exactly," Angus admitted. "I stumbled over an old dragon nest in the forest once and squashed some rotten eggs. Whew! Did they ever stink!" He waved a hand in front of his nose. "It took weeks to get the slimy goo off my boots."

"Then Torblad the Terrible and Baldrick the Bold...?" Wiglaf began.

Angus shook his head. "I am afraid my Uncle Mordred sometimes stretches the truth."

"The headmaster is your uncle?" Wiglaf exclaimed. "Imagine! So has anybody here ever killed a dragon?"

"Not yet," Eric piped up. "But soon someone shall—and that someone shall be me!"

Clang! Clang! A bell sounded and Eric slurped up the tail of his eel.

"Finish up," Angus advised Wiglaf.

"Stalking a Fire-Breather Class begins in five minutes. And it is way over in the East Tower."

Wiglaf stared at his fried eel on toast—now cold and gray. Then he left it on his plate and hurried after Angus and Eric.

Chapter 5

Wiglaf, Eric, and Angus rushed along the castle hallways until they came to a spiraling stone staircase. They ran up the steps, two at a time. When they reached the top of the East Tower, they were panting for breath.

Several boys stood at a window, pulling on a rope. Angus and Eric joined them.

Wiglaf, too, began to pull. "What are we raising?" he asked. "It is quite heavy."

"'Tis Sir Mort," Angus replied. "Our teacher. He has a hard time walking up stairs."

In a moment, Wiglaf saw why. A helmeted head appeared at the window. The boys reached out to pull their teacher in. And Sir Mort crashed to the classroom floor—wearing a full suit of armor.

The boys helped him to his feet.

"Stalking a fire-breather is no easy matter, lads," the old knight began lecturing as he lurched and clattered to the front of the room. "Dragons can hear you coming from miles away. Especially if you have on armor. Clanks something awful."

"Sir?" Eric called. "What about a dragon's sense of smell?"

"Oh, they smell all right." Sir Mort nodded thoughtfully. "Like old cheese, most of them. But I slew a dragon once that smelled exactly like my red wool socks when I wear 'em too long and the mold sets in."

Eric tried again. "I meant, can a dragon smell a dragon hunter?"

"Ah! Good question!" Sir Mort exclaimed. "That's how you learn, lads! By asking questions!" He looked around the room. "Are there any more questions?"

A tall, scared-looking boy raised his hand. "How close dare we stalk a dragon without danger?" he asked in a shaky voice.

"*That,*" Angus whispered to Wiglaf, "is Torblad the Terrible."

"How close!" Sir Mort exclaimed. "An excellent question. Excellent! You will go far, lad! Next question?"

Eric's hand shot up again. *He certainly is eager,* Wiglaf thought.

"Yesterday you said we must stalk different dragons in different ways," Eric said. "Can you give us an example?"

"Certainly I can." Sir Mort nodded, smiling. "Easy as pie."

Eric and the rest of the class waited. But Sir Mort only kept nodding and smiling.

"Sir?" Eric said at last. "Will you *show* us what you mean?"

"Good idea!" The old knight jangled to the center of the room.

"Take cave-dwelling dragons. They have excellent hearing," Sir Mort explained. "So they must be approached on the sly. I use what I call the Slide 'n' Glide. I stand sideways to the cave like this." Sir Mort turned sideways to the class. "And I slide my right foot out, like this." Sir Mort slid his right foot out.

Unfortunately, the old stone floors of the castle were far smoother than the ground outside a dragon's cave. Sir Mort's boot kept sliding and sliding...and sliding. Until the old knight clanked to the floor in a perfect split. His visor slammed down over his face.

"Hoist me up, lads!" Sir Mort cried in a muffled voice.

Eric and two other boys gripped their teacher under the arms and pulled him up.

"Ah, that's better." Sir Mort pushed his

visor back up. "Slippery devils, these boots. Reminds me of the time I stalked the dragon Fiffnir. Have I shown you the wound Fiffnir gave me? Nasty wound it is, too."

Sir Mort bent down. He began struggling to pull off the left boot of his armor.

In the distance a bell rang.

Angus spoke up. "Sir Mort, class is over."

"Devilish tight, this boot," Sir Mort grumbled.

"Sir, we must go to Slaying Class now," Angus continued. "Coach Plungett gets vexed if we are late."

"Go then, lads. Go!" Sir Mort said. "My wound will wait. Got it the year of the grasshopper plague. No, the year before. Couldn't have walked to Constantinople. Not with this wound. No, it must have been..."

Quietly, Wiglaf followed Angus and Eric and the other future dragon slayers down the spiral staircase. He was amazed at how much he had learned of dragon stalking in one short morning!

"Step it up, lads!" Coach Plungett called as Class I ran out into the castle yard. The large man's long brown pageboy-style hair blew gently in the breeze. "Ten laps around the castle," he ordered. "Can't kill a dragon if you're not in shape!"

By lap three, Eric was way ahead of the others. Wiglaf was way behind. He began to worry that slopping pigs and washing dishes had not prepared him well for dragon slaying.

But after the laps, the coach ordered the boys to take a deep breath and hold it for the count of fifty.

"If a dragon spews out poison," he told them, "the longer you can hold your breath, the better. Ready? And! One...two...three...."

Wiglaf smiled as he held his breath. Living

in the smelly hovel with his unwashed family had given him plenty of practice at this skill! He alone made it to the count of fifty.

"Good work!" Coach Plungett told him. "Now before we start slaying, why don't you give the DSA cheer for our new boy? Belt it out now, boys!"

At once, the whole class began shouting at the top of their lungs:

> *"Rooty-toot-ho! Rooty-toot-hey!*
> *We are the boys from DSA!*
> *We slay dragons, yes we do!*
> *Big ones! Bony ones! Fat ones, too!*
> *We slay dragons, young and old!*
> *We slay dragons, grab their gold!*
> *Yea! Yea! For good old DSA—Hey!"*

"Hey!" Coach clapped at the end of the cheer. "All right now, line up in front of Old Blodgett. Quickly, lads. Go on!"

Wiglaf and the others lined up in front of a

large dragon. It wasn't a real dragon, of course. Old Blodgett was only a wooden one covered with cloth and stuffed with straw.

"Slaying is the most important class here at DSA," Coach told the boys. "You can find a dragon. You can stalk a dragon. But if you cannot *slay* a dragon, you cannot get a hoard.

"Today we shall practice Slaying Method Number Seven, the Throat Thrust. Aim here." Coach Plungett pointed the tip of his sword just under Old Blodgett's chin where a target had been painted. "Not many scales in that spot. Watch me now!"

Coach Plungett faced the false dragon. He drew his weapon, galloped a few steps, and with a toss of his brown pageboy, thrust his sword deep into the dragon's neck.

Wiglaf cringed. He knew that no blood would spill from this dragon. Still his stomach did flip-flops.

Wiglaf watched with growing dread as each

boy took a turn stabbing the practice dragon. When his turn came, he drew Surekill, galloped toward the dragon, and stopped.

"Go on, boy!" Coach Plungett urged him.

Wiglaf backed up. He gripped Surekill more tightly. He stared at the target on the dragon's throat. He galloped forward again ...and stopped.

"Blazing King Ken's britches!" Coach cried. "Aim here!" He pointed at the target.

Wiglaf backed up once more. He swallowed. If he could not plunge his sword into this dummy dragon, what hope did he have of ever slaying a *real* one? Wiglaf took a step toward Old Blodgett. Then another. And another.

"I cannot watch!" Coach Plungett moaned. He turned away in disgust.

But Wiglaf kept on. Faster and faster he came. At the last minute, he closed his eyes.

"Haiii-yah!" he thrust Surekill up toward the dragon's chin.

But somehow Wiglaf missed. He went flying past the practice dragon and landed on a bale of straw. His eyes popped open. Around him, boys were hooting and pointing.

Wiglaf glanced at Surekill. His heart nearly stopped. He had missed the practice dragon. But he had speared some small, brown, furry creature! There it was, stuck on the end of his sword!

Why is everyone laughing, Wiglaf wondered, *when I have so cruelly killed a ...uh...?*

"I'll take that!" growled the coach.

Wiglaf looked up to see a very bald Coach Plungett snatch the hairy thing from the end of Surekill and angrily set it on his head.

Only then did Wiglaf understand what creature he had murdered. Coach Plungett's own brown pageboy wig!

Chapter 6

Wiglaf picked at his lunch of boiled eel on a bun. Coach Plungett was sure to give him an F in slaying now. He had messed up royally—and on his very first day of school.

"Come on, Wiglaf. Eat up!" Angus told him. "You do *not* want to be late for Mordred's class."

Mordred! Wiglaf shuddered. *What would the headmaster do to a new boy who had nearly slayed the slaying coach?*

With dark thoughts, Wiglaf followed Angus to a stone-walled classroom. As the boys sat down on a rickety bench, a huge man in a red cloak strode through the door. Thick black hair sprouted from his head. His violet eyes bulged like overripe plums.

"Atten-*tion!*" Mordred the Marvelous called.

The students leaped to their feet. Wiglaf did, too.

"At ease!" Mordred commanded.

The boys sat down.

"Let us review," the headmaster said. "Why are you here at Dragon Slayers' Academy?"

"To learn to slay evil dragons!" Eric called out at once. "To make the world safe for little children! To save villagers from—"

"Yes, yes," Mordred interrupted, holding up a hand heavy with gold rings. "That is all well and good. But what about yesterday's lesson? What did I say? Anyone? Baldrick?"

A small freckle-faced boy with a runny nose stood up. "We are here to learn how to get a dragon's golden hoard, sir! And bring it back to you, sir!"

"Correct!" Mordred grinned, showing a shiny gold front tooth. "To bring me gold! And"—he coughed—"to take some...a teeny bit...maybe...home to your"—he coughed again—"parents."

He cleared his throat. "Now, who remembers how to find a cave-dwelling dragon?"

Again, Eric was the first to answer. "Look for burned spots on shrubs and bushes!" he called. "And big footprints with three long toes!"

Mordred nodded. "And when you spot the dragon...what must you look out for?"

"Beware flames of death!" Eric shouted. "Beware a dragon's poison spit!"

"Correct, Eric." Mordred sighed and looked around. "Anyone *else?*"

"Beware the eyes that never close!" Eric called again. "Beware the knife-sharp teeth! Beware the powerful, lashing tail!"

"Thank you, *Eric,*" Mordred said. "Now,

what else must a dragon hunter know in order to *slay* such a beast?"

"How to talk to a dragon!" Eric called. "How to be brave!"

Mordred nodded. "Anything else?"

At last Eric was quiet. And so were all the other boys.

But Wiglaf had listened well to the minstrel's dragon tales. He knew there was one thing that Eric had not mentioned. Timidly, he raised his hand.

Mordred's bulging eyes lit on him. "Ah, the new boy! The one who scalped Coach Plungett!" The headmaster chuckled. "So, new boy, what else should a dragon hunter know?"

"A dragon's secret weakness?" Wiglaf said meekly.

"That's right!" Mordred's eyebrows shot up.

"Oh, everybody knows *that*," Eric complained.

"Let the new boy tell what he knows of dragon secrets, Eric," Mordred said. "Maybe you will learn something."

"From *him?*" Eric muttered. "Not likely."

"Well, new boy?" Mordred said. "Pray, tell us what you know!"

"I—I know very little..." Wiglaf began.

"See?" Eric cut in. "What did I tell you?"

But the headmaster ignored him. "New boy," he said, "know you the secret weakness of the dragon Gorzil?"

"No, sir," Wiglaf answered. "His weakness is still a secret."

"Too true." Mordred sighed sadly. "But it would be useful to know it. For Gorzil is rumored to be in the Dark Forest. My scout Yorick is there now. As soon as he finds Gorzil's cave, I shall send my best boys out to slay him. Slay him, and claim his great big golden hoard!"

These words were barely out of Mordred's

mouth when a small man burst into the classroom. Branches and leaves were tied to his tunic, as if he were trying to disguise himself as a bush.

"Yorick!" Mordred exclaimed. "Back so soon? What news from the Dark Forest?"

"My lord," Yorick began, "Gorzil has moved to a cave outside the village of Toenail."

"Toenail!" Torblad shrieked. "My family lives in Toenail!"

"Sit down, Torblad," Mordred snarled. "Go on, Yorick."

"My lord," Yorick said, "the Toenailians have brought Gorzil all their gold. Now he swears to burn Toenail to the ground unless a son and a daughter of the village are outside his cave tomorrow. Tomorrow at dawn, in time for breakfast!"

"Oh, that's nice of Gorzil," Torblad said, cheering up. "Having company for breakfast."

"You ninny!" Mordred cried. "They are to *be* his breakfast!" The headmaster turned back to his scout. "So! I shall send boys out to slay Gorzil this very afternoon!"

Then a look of horror crossed his face.

"Egad!" he exclaimed. "Class II and Class III just left on that blasted field trip to see the petrified dragon skeleton! That means I shall have to send Class I boys!"

"Pray, send me!" Eric cried, falling to his knees.

"Yes, yes," Mordred said. "But remember, we have a buddy system here. I'll need another volunteer." He looked around the room. "Anyone but Angus. If I sent you, I'd never hear the end of it from your mother. All right, who will it be?"

No hands went up.

"Come now," Mordred coaxed. "Gorzil is not so bad!"

Still no hands went up.

"My patience grows thin!" Mordred warned. Then his violet eyes lit upon Wiglaf.

"You! New boy!" he boomed. "You seem to know a fair bit about dragons. And I chanced to look at the register book at lunchtime. You never paid your seven pennies!"

"That is so," Wiglaf began. "But—" He stopped. He had promised Frypot to say not a word about their dishwashing deal.

"No buts!" Mordred cried. "You shall go with Eric! And you shall pay your seven pennies out of Gorzil's gold!"

"Aw, sir!" Eric cried. "Pray, pick someone else! Wiglaf has not even been here a whole day! He knows nothing of slaying!"

"*You* slay Gorzil, then!" Mordred shouted. "Let him pull the cart for the dragon's hoard. Now, be off! You must reach Gorzil's cave by dawn. What are you waiting for? Go!"

Chapter 7

"Ready, Wiglaf?" Eric called as he hurried toward the gate house.

Wiglaf was bent over, trying to fix a wobbly wheel on the hoard cart. He glanced up and was nearly blinded by the glare from Eric's slaying outfit.

Eric stood proudly before him in a gleaming silver helmet. He carried a broad silver shield. And a wide silver belt held his sword.

Wiglaf had only Surekill.

"What fine gear," Wiglaf told Eric.

"Yes," Eric agreed. "I sent away for it from the Sir Lancelot Fan Club catalog. Come! You shall pull the cart as Mordred said. Let us be off. My sword is itching to slay the dragon!"

Wiglaf began to slide back the great iron bolt on the gatehouse door. But a yell from Eric made him stop.

"Boar!" Eric cried. "Wild boar!"

Wiglaf turned to see Eric with his sword drawn and his shield up.

"Stand back!" Eric shouted. "I shall slay the charging beast!"

"What beast?" Wiglaf asked. Then he spotted something running toward them across the castle yard. It was Daisy!

"Eric, stop!" Wiglaf shouted. "Stop! That is my own pig, Daisy!"

Eric stopped and glumly lowered his sword. He jammed it back into its scabbard and stomped off, grumbling.

Wiglaf ran to Daisy.

"Iglaf-Way!" she squealed. "Ake-tay ee-may ith-way ou-yay!"

"I cannot, Daisy," Wiglaf said sadly. He squatted down beside her and scratched her bristly ears. "It is too dangerous. For I am off to hunt a dragon."

"Orzil-Gay?" Daisy's voice trembled.

Wiglaf nodded. "Who knows? Perhaps I shall return a hero." He tried to smile. "But if I do not"—he gulped—"if I do not return, I am sure Frypot will take good care of you. Now I—I must go. Farewell, best pig in the world!"

"Arewell-fay, Iglaf-Way!" Daisy called after him. "Ood-gay uck-lay!"

Wiglaf waved and hurried back to the gatehouse. Then he picked up the cart handle. "Let us be off," he said to Eric.

Wiglaf and Eric followed the trail down the hill from Dragon Slayers' Academy. Then they headed north on Huntsman's Path.

They walked beside the Swampy River all afternoon. Strange birds cried out from the stunted trees along the way. Hairy-legged spiders dropped down on them from over-hanging branches. Once an angry troll threatened them with his club. But Wiglaf was not afraid. The thought of facing Gorzil was so terrifying that nothing else bothered him.

Well, almost nothing.

"I shall slay Gorzil, no problem!" Eric announced for the two-hundredth time. "I shall plunge my sword into his throat. I shall twist it! Buckets of blood will gush from the dragon's steaming wound! Then I shall—"

"You know," Wiglaf broke in finally, "my sword was made for dragon slaying, too."

"That bent-up old thing?" Eric sneered.

Wiglaf nodded. "A wizard gave it to me," he explained. "When I say magic words, it will leap from my hand and obey."

Eric looked doubtful. "And just what are the magic words?"

"Uh...the wizard had forgotten," Wiglaf mumbled.

"It matters not," Eric scoffed as they came to a fork in Huntsman's Path. One path led to the village of Toenail. The other led into the Dark Forest. "For I shall slay this dragon with my own silvery sword. I shall cut Gorzil to ribbons! I shall—"

Suddenly, Eric stopped talking. He stared at the blackened leaves of a nearby shrub.

"Behold!" he cried. "This bush is scorched!"

Wiglaf bent down to take a closer look. "So it is," he agreed. "Could it be from the hot breath of a dragon?"

"How could it not? And look here!" Eric pointed to the ground. "Footprints!"

Wiglaf stared at a huge three-toed print in the path in front of them. "My, but these foot-prints are large!" he exclaimed.

"Come!" Eric said. "They will lead us to

Gorzil's cave. Hark!" he added. "What noise is that?"

Wiglaf listened. "It sounds like someone crying."

The sound grew louder. Then a boy and girl about Wiglaf and Eric's age came along on the path from Toenail. Tears streamed down their cheeks.

"What ails you, good travelers?" Eric called to them. "And how can we help?"

"Alackaday!" the boy wailed. "You cannot help us. No one can! My sister Zelda and I are on our way to Gorzil's cave!"

"Do you mean," Wiglaf began, "that you are the son and daughter of the village? That you are to be Gorzil's...breakfast?"

Zelda nodded. "I fear it is so. The Toenail village masters held a lottery. And alas— Gawain and I won!"

"If only a brave knight would slay Gorzil

and save us!" Gawain said. "But there is no hope of that."

Eric yanked his sword from its scabbard and held it high in the air.

"Fear not, young friends," he cried. "Eric the Dragon Slayer is at your service!"

Gawain and Zelda stared at him.

"You?" Zelda said.

Eric nodded.

"You are but a boy!" she scoffed.

Eric sniffed. "I am first in my class at Dragon Slayers' Academy," he replied. "I shall slay Gorzil—no sweat!"

"Do you know how many brave knights have tried and perished in his flames?" Gawain asked.

"Um...no. But—" Eric began.

"Gorzil will toast you like a marshmallow!" Zelda declared. "Unless," she added, "you come up with a clever plan."

"A plan?" Wiglaf said. "What kind of—"

"Change clothes with us," Zelda cut in. "Disguise yourselves as the son and the daughter of Toenail and catch Gorzil off guard!"

At first, Eric looked doubtful. Then he began to smile. "Yes!" he exclaimed. "I can see it now! At dawn, *we* shall appear at the mouth of Gorzil's cave, dressed in your clothing. Gorzil will never suspect that behind my back I have a sword! When the dragon opens his jaws to eat me, I shall whip out my sword and plunge it deep into his throat. His whole body will shudder and—"

"But Eric," Wiglaf broke in. "How can one of *us* pass for a *daughter* of the village?"

But Eric was already taking off his helmet. "Worry not, Wiglaf," he said. "Just be quick and give your tunic to Gawain. Here, Zelda. Take my Sir Lancelot armor." Eric handed the girl his helmet and chainmail. "As soon as we are dressed in their clothes," Eric told Wiglaf, "we shall go thitherward to carry out our plan!"

Chapter 8

The sun dawned on Wiglaf and Eric outside the mouth of Gorzil's cave. With trembling fingers, Wiglaf finished tying his lucky rag to Surekill's hilt. If ever he needed luck, it was now!

Wiglaf adjusted Gawain's baggy tunic and trousers. Then he glanced over at Eric, who was wearing Zelda's sky-blue dress. His brown hair peeked out from under her white lace cap.

"I was wrong to think you would not pass for a daughter of the village, Eric," Wiglaf said.

Eric only nodded.

"That lace cap suits you," Wiglaf went on. "If I were a dragon, I should believe you were a girl—and a fetching one, at that."

"Enough!" Eric snapped. "Keep your thoughts on Gorzil!"

Just then a cloud of smoke billowed out of the cave, and a voice inside boomed, "I SMELL BREAKFAST!"

Wiglaf and Eric hid their swords behind their backs as a huge, green, snakelike head poked out from the smoke. The dragon's eyes blazed orange. Steam rose from his jaws. Yellow slime dripped from his nose. Wiglaf had never seen anything so hideous.

So this was Gorzil! Wiglaf thought back to the minstrel's tale. He gripped his sword more tightly. He hoped that Gorzil would not soon be using Surekill for his toothpick!

Gorzil puffed two smoke rings from his nose. "What luck!" he exclaimed. "Here are a

tasty little son and daughter of the village. And here is Gorzil, hungry for breakfast! Daughter, have you any last words to say to Gorzil?"

Eric took a step forward. He whispered something. But even Wiglaf could not hear what it was.

"What? What?" Gorzil said. "Speak up, girl!" But Eric only whispered again.

The dragon stepped out from the cave. Slime trickled from his nose. It spattered on the ground in greasy yellow puddles. He lowered his head close to Eric. "Now Gorzil can hear better. What did you say, my delicious cookie?"

"I AM NOT YOUR COOKIE, GORZIL!" Eric shouted into the dragon's ear. "I AM YOUR WORST NIGHTMARE!" And he whipped his sword from behind his back.

An angry red crest rose from Gorzil's head.

Sparks shot from his nose. They scorched the hem of Eric's dress. Then Gorzil raised the tip of his tail over his head and whacked Eric's sword out of his hand.

Wiglaf and Eric watched it sail off into the woods.

"Uh-oh," said Eric. He ducked behind a nearby boulder. "Quick, Wiglaf!" he called. "Draw your sword!"

Wiglaf stared up at the monster before him. He tried to remember what he had learned in his one-and-only slaying class. But Gorzil was no dummy dragon with a target painted under his chin. He was the real thing!

With a quivering hand, Wiglaf brought Surekill out from behind his back.

The dragon gazed at the rusty thing and chuckled.

"Surekill," Wiglaf said, "slay the dragon!"

Surekill did not move.

"Surekill!" Wiglaf tried again. "Do the dragon in!"

Surekill made no thrust.

Yellow flames began to flicker from Gorzil's nostrils.

"Surekill!" Wiglaf yelled. "HELP!"

In the blink of an eye, the sword leaped out of Wiglaf's hand. It glowed red hot as it soared up, up into the air. Gorzil stopped flaming. Wiglaf and Eric and the dragon all stared as Surekill rose higher and higher into the clouds. They waited for it to reappear. But the sword had vanished.

At last, Gorzil fixed his gaze back on Wiglaf. "Too bad," he chortled. "Now it is breakfast time!"

Gorzil opened his terrible jaws. Any second, Wiglaf knew, lightning bolts would strike him!

If only I had more time! he thought. *Time*

enough to discover Gorzil's secret weakness! But how? Wiglaf racked his brain. But he could think of nothing. Nothing!

At last, Wiglaf opened his mouth, and over Gorzil's thundering roar, he yelled the first thing that came to his mind: "Knock! Knock!"

Instantly, the thunder stopped.

"A joke!" the dragon cried. "There's nothing Gorzil likes better than a good joke! Breakfast can wait. All right....Who's there?"

"Lettuce," Wiglaf managed.

"Lettuce?" Gorzil snorted a puff of smoke. "Lettuce? Gorzil can guess! Easy! Oh, foo. Lettuce who?"

"Lettuce alone!" Wiglaf answered.

"Oooooh," Gorzil groaned. "That was a bad joke."

"Really bad," Eric called from behind the rock.

"Gorzil *hates* bad jokes," the dragon added.

In fact, Wiglaf thought that the dragon looked slightly ill.

"Try again, son of the village," Gorzil ordered. "Tell Gorzil another joke. But make it a good one!"

"All right," Wiglaf said. "Knock! Knock!"

The dragon perked up. "Gorzil will get this one! Who's there?"

"Arthur!" cried Wiglaf.

"Arthur? Hmm. Oh, yes! Oh, poo. Arthur who?"

Wiglaf answered, "Arthur any dragons uglier than you?"

"Aghh!" Gorzil cried. "That was even worse!"

Wiglaf noticed that Gorzil's bright orange eyes had faded. His scales were no longer a brilliant green. The dragon looked the way Wiglaf felt when he heard too many of Fergus's knock-knocks: Sick.

Suddenly Wiglaf had a hunch. Could it be?

His heart began to race with excitement.

"Knock! Knock!" Wiglaf said again.

"Who's there?" Gorzil mumbled.

"Howard!" called Wiglaf.

"How—Howard who?" Gorzil asked weakly.

Wiglaf yelled, "Howard you like to hear another rotten joke?"

"Another? Uggghh!" The dragon gasped for air. He clutched at his scaly chest with his claws.

Quickly, Wiglaf struck again: "Knock! Knock!"

"Who...there?" Gorzil's head was drooping now.

"Ivan!" Wiglaf shouted.

"Iv...whooo...?" Gorzil's legs buckled under him. He hit the ground.

"Ivan to stay alive!" Wiglaf cried.

That did it. Gorzil's chest heaved. His tail lashed one final time and was still. His tongue flopped out the side of his mouth and lay in a puddle of yellow drool. Then, with a thunderous poof, Gorzil's body exploded into a cloud of dragon dust.

Eric hiked up his skirt and ran through the dust to Wiglaf's side.

"By Lancelot's lance!" he exclaimed. "Gorzil is dead!"

Then all at once, Wiglaf heard a wild roar. He turned to see hundreds of cheering villagers popping out from behind rocks and trees. Villagers who had come to watch them fight the dragon!

Joyfully, the villagers began rushing toward them. Wiglaf brushed the dragon dust from his tunic. He readied himself to be lifted up onto their shoulders. To be carried through Toenail, a hero!

"Out of me way!" a villager shouted, gruffly shoving past him. A stampede of villagers followed on his heels.

Wiglaf and Eric had to leap behind a

boulder or be trampled as the whole crowd charged straight into the cave—straight for Gorzil's hoard.

As the two dragon hunters stood staring, a flash lit the sky. Wiglaf looked up just in time to see Surekill tumble from the clouds—down into a clump of weeds.

"Nice try Surekill," said Wiglaf.

Chapter 9

"**D**id the villagers have to grab every last bit of Gorzil's hoard?" Eric grumbled.

By this time, Eric had fetched his sword, and Wiglaf and Eric had found Gawain and Zelda and switched clothes again. Eric told Zelda he was sorry about the burned spots on her dress. But she was so loaded with gold, she did not seem to mind at all.

Now Wiglaf and Eric were back on the path to DSA. This time Eric pulled the cart.

"I am all for taking from the rich and giving to the poor," Eric went on. "But could not the villagers have left us a few gold coins?

How shall we ever face Mordred empty-handed?"

"Gorzil stole from the villagers," Wiglaf reminded him. "It seems only fair that they should get their gold back."

"I suppose," muttered Eric. And with a sigh he dragged the cart over a rocky patch of ground.

"Are you sure you want to pull the cart?" Wiglaf asked him.

"It is the least I can do," Eric told Wiglaf. "For in truth, you did slay the mighty dragon."

Wiglaf blushed on hearing Eric's words. "I could never have done it without you, Eric," he said. "It was a clever plan—and you surely fooled Gorzil into thinking you were a girl."

For a moment, Eric was silent. Then he stopped and turned to Wiglaf. "There is something I should like to tell you," he said gravely.

"Pray, tell," Wiglaf answered.

"'Tis a secret," Eric warned him. "Will you swear to keep it?"

"I swear it on my sword," Wiglaf promised. He lifted Surekill into the air.

"My real name," Eric told him, "is Erica."

"Egad!" Wiglaf exclaimed. "Your parents gave you a girl's name?"

"No! I *am* a girl, you ninny. In fact, I am a princess. Princess Erica, daughter of Queen Barb and King Ken."

Wiglaf's mouth dropped open.

"I always longed for a life of adventure," Erica explained. "When I saw the notice for Dragon Slayers' Academy, I begged my parents to let me go. At last they agreed. But when I arrived at school, Frypot said Mordred would never admit a girl. It was good old Frypot's plan to dress me as a boy.

He keeps my secret. And in return, I empty his eel traps."

"Zounds!" Wiglaf exclaimed. Then he added, "Forgive me, your highness."

"None of that highness stuff!" the princess growled. She drew her silvery sword and waved it at Wiglaf. "You must call me only Eric! And do not slip up! No one at school must know my secret. Not until I get my Dragon Slayers' Academy diploma. If you tell anyone, I shall make you very, very sorry!"

"I shall never say a word," Wiglaf promised. "And if I do, you may tell *my* secret."

"Your secret?" asked Erica.

"See this lucky rag tied to the hilt of my sword?" Wiglaf asked. "It is...uh...the last bit of my baby blanket."

Erica smiled. "Indeed! That is not something that you would want to get around." She gave a yank to the cart handle and started down the path again.

"Now," Erica went on, "let us go over the story we shall tell back at DSA. Since we have no gold, we must make the most of our adventure."

"A fine idea," Wiglaf agreed.

"I think," Erica began, "that we shall start by telling how I bravely lured Gorzil out of his cave. And how I scared him near to death when I brandished my silvery sword! Then, when he least expected it..."

As Eric—make that Erica—talked on, Wiglaf let his own thoughts wander. He had become a hero—just as the minstrel had said he would. And without spilling a single drop of blood!

Daisy would be so proud of me, Wiglaf thought. And wouldn't Fergus and Molwena and his twelve unwashed brothers be surprised when they learned that he was indeed Wiglaf of Pinwick, Dragon Slayer!

Dragon Slayers' Academy 2

REVENGE OF
THE DRAGON LADY

For Jim, my darling boy

—K.H. McM.

REVENGE OF
THE DRAGON LADY

By K.H. McMullan
Illustrated by Bill Basso

GROSSET & DUNLAP • NEW YORK

Library of Congress Cataloging-in-Publication Data

McMullan, K.H.
    Revenge of the dragon lady / by K.H. McMullan ; illustrated by Bill Basso.
      p. cm. — (Dragon Slayers' Academy ; 2)
    Summary: After accidentally killing a dragon, Wiglaf hopes his friends at Dragon Slayers'
Academy will be able to help him prove himself a hero when he faces that dragon's mother,
Seetha, the Beast from the East.
    [1. Dragons—Fiction. 2. Schools—Fiction. 3. Courage—Fiction.]
I. Basso, Bill, ill. II. Title. III. Series: McMullan, K.H.
Dragon Slayers' Academy ; 2.
PZ7.M47879Re 1997   97-31171
[Fic]—dc21   CIP
                                           AC

ISBN   0-448-42289-1   A B C D E F G H I J

Chapter I

Wiglaf sat in the cold dining hall of Dragon Slayers' Academy. He stared at the slimy jellied eels on his plate.

"Yuck!" he said to his friend Erica. "I'm sick of having eels for breakfast!"

Erica brushed a clump of brown hair out of her eyes. "Get over it, Wiglaf," she told him.

"I know, I know," Wiglaf said miserably. "The castle moat is swarming with eels. And as long as our headmaster can get eels for free, he will have Frypot cook us eels for breakfast, lunch, and dinner."

With her bread, Erica sopped up every last drop of dark green eel juice on her plate. She popped the bread into her mouth.

How could she stand it? Wiglaf wondered.

"Mmmm," Erica said. "I love it!"

Erica loved everything about DSA—including the eels. She didn't even mind emptying the eel traps each morning. Wiglaf was pretty sure that was one of the reasons she had won the Future Dragon Slayer of the Month Medal.

Wiglaf tasted a small bite of tail. Disgusting! He pushed his plate of eels across the table.

"Here, Erica," he said. "Have mine."

"Shhh! It's *Eric*, remember?" Erica looked around the dining hall to see whether anyone at the other tables had heard. "If Mordred discovers I'm a girl and kicks me out of school, it will be *your* fault!"

"Sorry," Wiglaf said.

"You're the only one who knows my secret," Erica went on. "If you tell anyone, I swear, I'll whack off your head! I'll plunge my sword into your gut! Your blood will—"

"All right, Eric!" Wiglaf cut in quickly. "I get your meaning."

Wiglaf knew Erica was dying to slay a dragon and become a hero. But did she have to go on and on about plunging her sword into *him*?

Wiglaf wanted to be a hero, too. Heroes were brave and bold. If he were a hero, no one would tease him about being small for his age. Or about his carrot-colored hair. So Wiglaf had left home, with his pet pig, Daisy, at his side. He had come to Dragon Slayers' Academy to learn how to kill dragons and become a hero.

There was only one small problem with his plan.

Wiglaf couldn't stand the sight of blood.

"Wiglaf! Eric!" someone called from across the dining hall.

Wiglaf looked up. He saw Angus, the head-master's nephew, running toward their table.

Angus was plump and sandy-haired. He never ran when he could walk. He never walked when he could sit. So Wiglaf knew he must have important news.

"Angus!" Erica exclaimed. "What is it?"

Angus stood by the Class I table, catching his breath. "Uncle Mordred is having a tantrum," he said.

"That's nothing new," Wiglaf pointed out. Mordred was always yelling at him because of what had happened with a dragon named Gorzil. Wiglaf and Erica had been sent off to kill Gorzil. And Wiglaf *had* killed him. But only by accident. He had stumbled upon Gorzil's secret weakness—bad jokes. And four bad jokes later, Gorzil was history. But Mordred didn't yell about how he had killed the dragon. He yelled about how Wiglaf had let some greedy villagers take all of Gorzil's gold.

"But this is a major tantrum," Angus was saying. "Mordred just heard about a boy from Dragon Exterminators' Prep. He killed a dragon and brought his headmaster all the dragon's gold. Uncle Mordred is screaming and yelling that one of us had better slay a dragon soon.

One of us must bring him some gold, or—"

"Angus!" Wiglaf cried. "Duck!"

Angus ducked. A fat jellied eel flew over his head. It landed in Erica's lap.

Erica leaped to her feet. "Hey! Who threw that?" she called.

"Me!" yelled a boy from the Class II table. "What are you going to do about it?"

"You will see!" Erica yelled back. The Future Dragon Slayer of the Month loved a good food fight as much as any other DSA student. She snatched up an eel from Wiglaf's plate. She threw it. "Bull's-eye!" she yelled as it hit its mark.

At once the air was thick with flying eels.

Wiglaf grinned. Moments like this were the best part of being at Dragon Slayers' Academy! He grabbed an eel. He threw it across the room. Then he joined in the chant that boys at the Class III table had started: "No more eel! No more eel!"

Soon the dining hall was filled with the sound of feet stomping and voices chanting: "No more eel! No more eel!"

Wiglaf picked up the last eel from his plate. He eyed the life-sized bust of Mordred that stood on a post by the door. The headmaster's thick hair, his big popping eyes, and his wide smile had been carved into stone.

Wiglaf took aim. "This one is for you, Mordred!" he yelled. Then he hurled his eel at the stone head.

But at that very moment, the flesh-and-blood headmaster walked through the dining hall door.

Wiglaf stared in horror as his eel hit the real Mordred's face with a mighty splat!

Chapter 2

The eel stuck to Mordred's forehead. Green eel juice dripped into his angry violet eyes. It trickled down his cheeks to his beard.

"You!" Mordred roared at Wiglaf. "I should have known!" He ripped the flattened fish from his forehead. He threw it over his shoulder.

"You!" Mordred thundered. He glared at Wiglaf. "The only DSA pupil ever to slay a dragon! But did you bring me Gorzil's gold? You did NOT!"

"I-I tried to, sir," Wiglaf said. "But the villagers ran into Gorzil's cave, and—"

"Excuses! Excuses!" Mordred shouted. "And

you never paid your tuition! You still owe me seven pennies!"

"That is true," Wiglaf began. "But you see, sir, my family has no money. And my father wanted me to sell my pig. But I—"

"And now you go and hit me with an eel!" Mordred cut in. "As soon as you pay your seven pennies, I shall kick you out of school!"

Mordred took a big red handkerchief from his pocket. He wiped the last of the eel juice from his face.

"But, now," he continued, "it's detention for one and all!" He pointed a fat gold-ringed finger toward the stairs. "To the dungeon! March!"

The DSA students lined up. They marched down three flights of stone steps. One by one, the pupils filed into the cold, damp dungeon.

When everyone was inside, Mordred slammed the door. He lit a pair of torches on the wall.

"Angus! Come here!" the headmaster barked. "The rest of you, sit!"

Angus stepped forward. Wiglaf and the rest of the students sat down on the hard floor.

Mordred gave Angus a jar of quills and several bottles of ink. "Pass these around," he ordered. "Then give out the parchment."

Angus obeyed in silence.

At last everyone had writing supplies.

"Write down all one hundred rules for future dragon slayers," Mordred said. "Neatly, now. No cross-outs or ink blots allowed."

Erica's hand shot up. "Is there a prize for whoever finishes first?" she asked.

"No, Eric. This is a punishment." Mordred frowned at the hourglass he wore strapped to his wrist. "You have two hours. Begin!"

Two hours! Wiglaf's heart sank as he dipped his quill into an ink bottle. He wrote:

100 Rules for Future Dragon Slayers

1. A future dragon slayer will gladly lay

down his life to get gold for Mordred.
2. A future dragon slayer never
complains—especially in letters home.
3. A future dragon slayer eats what is on
his plate—no matter what it looks like.
4. Or tastes like.
5. Or smells like.

Five down, Wiglaf thought. Only ninety-five to go. He glanced over at Erica's paper. How had she written eighteen rules already?

6. A future dragon slayer must keep his
sword sharp and ready for action.

Swords! thought Wiglaf. *That's all anybody at DSA cares about.* He had killed a dragon! So what if he hadn't used his sword. He had done it with jokes. But shouldn't that count for something? It didn't seem to. Nobody seemed to think slaying a dragon with jokes was one bit heroic. Wiglaf sighed. How was he ever going to become a hero?

Wiglaf had just dipped his quill into the ink again when he heard a fluttering noise. He and several others looked up. At the barred window of the dungeon they saw the face of a giant bird!

Mordred looked up, too.

"Zounds!" he yelped. "A bird of evil omen has come to devour us all!"

"My lord!" the bird called. "It is I, your scout, Yorick." He reached out a wing tip and pulled off his big yellow beak. "See?"

"Yorick!" Mordred cried. "Quick! Come down here! Bring me your news!"

A moment later, Yorick waddled into the dungeon. He was covered from head to toe with grimy gray feathers.

"My lord," Yorick said, "I have been spying for you on Buzzard's Peak."

"Ah!" Mordred nodded. "So that explains your buzzard disguise."

Wiglaf thought Yorick looked like a huge pigeon. But he kept his thought to himself.

"My lord," Yorick went on, "a black cloud is blowing in from the east."

Mordred rolled his violet eyes. "I don't pay you to bring me weather reports, Yorick!"

"My lord," Yorick said, "this is no ordinary cloud. It is a cloud of smoke."

"Egad!" Mordred exclaimed. His eyes lit up with excitement. "You cannot mean..."

"I do, my lord," Yorick continued. "A dragon is headed this way. My sources say it is a she-dragon. She is hunting down the warrior who slew her son."

"*Oh!*" Mordred cried. "There is nothing more terrible than an angry mother dragon! I wonder who this unlucky warrior can be?" He tapped his gold-ringed fingers on his chin. "Sir Freddy Headwhacker? No, I'll bet it's that old rascal, Sir Percy Smackbottom."

"My lord," Yorick said, "they say it is the warrior who killed the dragon Gorzil."

"Gorzil?" Angus gasped. "Wiglaf! The dragon is coming after you!"

Chapter 3

Wiglaf suddenly had a bad feeling in his stomach. And it wasn't from the jellied eel.

"M-m-m-me?" he said.

"You, my boy!" Mordred exclaimed happily. "What luck!"

"Luck?" Wiglaf said. His heart pounded with fear. "It doesn't seem lucky to me."

At this moment, becoming a hero didn't seem so important. Staying alive—that's what mattered.

"Just think—a dragon coming right to my front door!" Mordred smiled. His gold front tooth shone in the torchlight. "Where there's a dragon, there are sure to be piles and piles of

GOLD close by! Oh, just thinking of it boggles the mind!"

"Sir?" Erica called out. "Remember how you sent Wiglaf and me out to kill Gorzil? Well, Wiglaf never even touched that dragon. He killed him by accident!"

"That's true, sir," Wiglaf added quickly.

"See?" Erica said. "Wiglaf even says it's true! But I was ready to kill Gorzil the right way! I had drawn my sword! I was ready to cut off Gorzil's ugly head! By all rights, it's me that Gorzil's mother should be hunting down!"

"Eric," Mordred said patiently. "Who turned Gorzil into dragon dust?"

"Well, uh...Wiglaf," Erica admitted. "But—"

Mordred shook a finger at his student. "You must not be jealous of the feats of others," he scolded.

Erica slumped down. "Sorry, sir," she said.

"Are we clear on this?" Mordred asked. "The dragon is after Wiglaf? And Wiglaf alone?"

Wiglaf let out a groan.

"Yes, sir," Erica answered glumly.

"Good." Mordred turned back to his scout. "Yorick," he said, "when will the dragon be here?"

"My lord," Yorick replied, "I multiplied the length of the smoky cloud by its width. Then I subtracted the wind speed—"

"Spit it out, man!" Mordred yelled. "When?"

"My lord," Yorick said, "when the noon bell rings on Friday, Seetha will arrive."

"Friday!" Wiglaf cried. "But that's only two days from—"

"Hush!" Mordred clamped a hand over Wiglaf's mouth. "Yorick! What did you say the dragon's name was?"

"Seetha, my lord," said Yorick.

The smile faded from Mordred's face. "Seetha? The Beast from the East? No!" he wailed. "It can't be! This is too, too horrible!"

Wiglaf started shaking. Seetha must be awful indeed to make Mordred act this way!

"Yorick!" Mordred cried. "I beg you! Say her name is Deetha! Or Queetha! Or Loreetha!"

Yorick only shook his head.

"No dragon has ever come to DSA!" Mordred exclaimed. "Now one is coming. Any dragon in the world would bring along its golden hoard. Any dragon but one. And that one is Seetha!"

"She has no gold?" Angus asked.

"No!" Mordred cried. Tears sprang to his violet eyes. "Seetha cares nothing for gold! All she cares about is killing. She does it for fun!"

"For fun?" Wiglaf squeaked. He started shaking harder. And his teeth began to chatter. "But what does she...How does she..."

"Oh, Seetha loves fun and games," Mordred said. "She plays with her victims for hours before she makes her kill. But she has no gold!" he moaned. "Woe is me! No gold!"

He waved a hand toward the dungeon door. "Go, boys. Detention is over. Just go. Leave me to my sorrow!"

Erica jumped to her feet. "Sir!" she cried. "What you need is a DSA cheer!" She turned to the rest of the students. "Let's do *Look Out, Dragons!* Really yell it now. Ready? And!"

Then everyone—everyone but Wiglaf—marched out of the dungeon shouting:

> *"Look out, dragons! Here we come!*
> *DSA! That's where we're from!*
> *Will we slay you?*
> *Yes! We will!*
> *Here we come to kill! Kill! Kill!"*

Chapter 4

"Gorzil's mother is coming to get me!" Wiglaf moaned. He lay on his cot that afternoon during rest hour. "Oh, I'm toast!"

"Pipe down, Wiglaf!" said a tall boy in a cot by the door. "Some of us are trying to rest."

"Go blow your nose, Torblad!" Erica snapped. She sat on the edge of Wiglaf's cot. "I hate to think what you would be like if a dragon was hunting you down!"

Wiglaf moaned louder. He turned to a picture he had drawn of his pig, Daisy, curled up in her cozy bed in the DSA henhouse.

"My poor Daisy!" Wiglaf said. "When I'm gone, she will be all alone in the world."

"That's the least of your worries," Angus offered from his cot on the other side of

Wiglaf's. "Here. This will make you feel better." He broke off a piece of his Camelot Crunch Bar. He handed it to Wiglaf. "Maybe you should run away before Seetha gets here," he added. "Maybe you should go home."

"I can't." Wiglaf passed the candy on to Erica. He was not hungry. "My father told me not to come home without a pile of gold. And he has a temper as bad as Mordred's."

"Uncle Mordred isn't so tough," Angus said. "You should see him when my Aunt Lobelia comes for a visit. She is his big sister. And boy, does she ever boss him around. Once—"

"Angus! Stop talking about your aunt!" Erica broke in. "We have to help Wiggie figure out how he's going to kill Seetha. Look."

Erica reached into her pocket. She brought out two small lead figures. One was a tiny Sir Lancelot. The other was a tiny dragon.

"Here is how *The Sir Lancelot Handbook* says to do it," she said. "'Take up your sword. Smite the dragon on the noggin!'"

Erica made the little Lancelot bonk the little dragon three times on the head.

"*Arrrrgh!*" she wailed. She made the little dragon flop down on its side. "I'm done for!"

"But Seetha won't hold still while I try to smite her!" Wiglaf said. "And let's face it," he added, "I'm no Sir Lancelot."

"I'll say," Erica snorted.

"What you need to do," Angus said, "is find out Seetha's secret weakness. If you can do that, you won't have to smite her."

"I was lucky to have guessed Gorzil's weakness," Wiglaf said. "But what are the chances of that happening again?"

"You don't need luck," Angus said. "You need the right book. There are loads of dragon books in the DSA library."

"What?" Erica exclaimed. "DSA has a library?"

"We have a free period after rest hour," Wiglaf said. "Let's hit the library!"

Chapter 5

BONG! The bell ending rest hour rang.

Angus led Wiglaf and Erica out to the castle yard. Afternoon classes had just begun.

Sir Mort's Stalking Class was learning how to sneak up on a dragon from behind.

Coach Plungett was teaching his Slaying Class the Gut Stab on the practice dragon.

The boys in Frypot's Scrubbing Class were down on their hands and knees washing the castle steps. Mordred claimed that scrubbing was an important skill for future dragon slayers. But Wiglaf never understood exactly why.

The three reached the South Tower. They

ran up a winding stone staircase to the DSA library.

Brother Dave, the librarian, looked up as they walked in. He had a round face and small, round glasses. He wore a brown monk's robe.

"Good day, Angus!" Brother Dave exclaimed. "I see thou hast brought some friends here with thee on this fine afternoon!"

Brother Dave's order of monks had to do good deeds. The deeds had to be so hard that most people could never do them. Brother Dave had decided to become the librarian at DSA, where few of the students—and none of the teachers—had ever read a whole book.

"Art thou here to work on a report that shall keep thee in the library many hours?" Brother Dave asked. He looked hopeful.

"No," Wiglaf replied. "I'm not here about school work...."

"Oh! A child who reads for pleasure!" Brother Dave clasped his hands to his heart. He looked thrilled. "Maybe thou would like

The King Who Couldn't Sleep by Eliza Wake. A great story. Or perhaps thou might try *Into the Dark Forest* by Hugo First. Or, if thou likes poetry—"

"Brother Dave?" Angus cut in. "My friend Wiglaf here is in trouble. He is going to be roasted in two days unless we can get some facts about the dragon Seetha."

"Seetha?" Brother Dave gasped. "Canst thou mean the Beast from the East?"

"You've heard of her, too?" Wiglaf cried. "Oh, please, Brother Dave! I need a book that will tell me Seetha's secret weakness!"

Brother Dave grew thoughtful. "I know of only one book that might tell thee that," he said. "Let me get it." He dashed off and returned with *The Encyclopedia of Dragons*.

Wiglaf gladly took the big book from the monk. Here in his very hands he might be holding the key to Seetha's downfall. Who knew? Perhaps he would live to see Saturday after all!

Wiglaf turned the pages to the "S" section. He kept turning. At last he saw the name *Seetha*. A hideous face stared back at him from the page.

"Whoa!" Angus exclaimed. "That is one scary dragon lady!"

A horn grew out of Seetha's head. Pink curly tentacles sprouted from the base of the horn. They hung down over her yellow eyes. A long tongue curved out of her fang-filled mouth.

"She looks mean, all right," Erica said. "Where do you think you will plunge your sword, Wiggie? Here, in Seetha's neck? Or in her heart? Or maybe in her big, fat gut? Or—"

"Stop!" Wiglaf said. "Let us see what the book has to say."

What it had to say was this:

Full name: *Seetha von Flambé*
Also known as: *The Beast from the East*
Husband: *Fangol von Flambé*
(slain by Sir Gristle McThistle in 1143 A.D.)

Children: *3,684*

Appearance:

    Scales: *swamp green*

    Horn: *burnt orange*

    Eyes: *yes*

    Teeth: *disgusting!*

Age: *one thousand and counting*

Most often heard saying:

    "Let's go torch a wizard's tower!"

Best known for:

    smelling bad...really, REALLY bad

Biggest surprise:

    she's not into gold

Hobby: *playing fun killing games*

Favorite thing in all the world:

    Son #92, Gorzil, her darling boy

"Oh, I'm doomed!" cried Wiglaf.

"This does not look good for you, Wiggie," Erica said.

The three friends read on. Wiglaf turned the page. Suddenly they all gasped. At the top of the page, it said:

Secret weakness:

> *Knights who know say Seetha's fatal*
> *weakness is ba—*

Ink had spilled over the page. The rest of the word was covered with a thick black blob.

"Ba— what?" Wiglaf cried. "I need to know!"

Angus held the page up to the burning candle on Brother Dave's desk. "I can't make out the rest of the word," he said. "But maybe Seetha's weakness is the same as Gorzil's—bad jokes."

Erica shook her head. "No two dragons have the same secret weakness," she said. "I read that in *The Sir Lancelot Handbook*."

"But ba— could be so many things," Angus pointed out. "Bananas. Ballads. Barbecued beef on a bun."

"Looks like you are going to have to slay this dragon the old-fashioned way—with your sword," Erica told Wiglaf. "If I were you, I'd ask Coach Plungett for some extra help in slashing and bashing."

Wiglaf nearly gagged at the thought. "But I'm no good at that stuff!"

"If I were thee," the monk said, gazing down at Wiglaf, "I would start saying my prayers!"

Chapter 6

"Ba— could be bait," Angus said. "Or balloons. Or—"

"We have to go," Erica cut in. "Or we'll be late for Slaying. Thanks, Brother Dave!"

"Ba— could be banjos or back rubs or badminton," Angus went on as they left the library.

"I'm doomed!" Wiglaf exclaimed. "Doomed!"

"Stop being so gloomy!" Erica ordered. "Even if the worst happens, death by dragon is a noble way to die."

"But I don't want to die!" Wiglaf cried.

"Ba— could be baskets," Angus kept on as they ran down the steps. "Or baboons. Or battle-axes."

"It could be a thousand different things," Wiglaf said. "Oh, I wish I could just disappear!"

Angus stopped suddenly.

"Keep moving!" Erica said.

"Disappear," Angus said. He began walking slowly down the steps again. "That gives me an idea. Maybe my Aunt Lobelia could help you, Wiglaf. For there are those who say"— he dropped his voice— "that Lobelia is a sorceress."

"Do *you* think she is?" Wiglaf asked.

Angus nodded. "My mother is always saying that Lobelia can transform people. That she works wonders on them. And you know what?" He smiled. "Mordred keeps a room for Lobelia here in the castle."

Wiglaf stopped dead in his tracks.

"Move!" Erica cried. "You don't want to be late, do you?"

But Wiglaf didn't move. "Angus, do you think Lobelia has something in her room that might transform me?" he asked. "Something to make me disappear for a few days?"

"She might." Angus grinned. "Let's go see. I happen to know that Uncle Mordred keeps the key to her room on a nail over his desk."

"Sneaking in is against DSA rules," Erica reminded them. She fingered her Future Dragon Slayer of the Month Medal which she wore on a ribbon around her neck. "But don't worry," she added. "If you two go, I won't tell. Now, out of my way. I'm going to Slaying." Erica pushed past Wiglaf and Angus. She hurried down the stairs.

Ten minutes later, Angus lifted the latch and slowly opened Mordred's office door. He peeked inside.

"All clear," he whispered.

Wiglaf walked into the office behind Angus. He didn't want to think what the headmaster would do to them if he caught them there.

The boys made their way to the key. They had just reached it when a low moan startled them.

Wiglaf turned. Yikes! There was Mordred! Angus hadn't seen him because he was lying down on his velvet couch.

Mordred had put on a pair of red pajamas. Tears rolled down his cheeks. He was mumbling to himself, "A dragon with no gold. Alas! The thought of it makes me ill!"

Wiglaf sighed with relief. Mordred was suffering far too much to notice them.

Angus lifted the key silently off its nail. Then the boys left the office.

In the hallway, Angus burst out laughing. "What a baby Mordred is!" he exclaimed. "Say, maybe that's Seetha's weakness—babies!"

"Give it up, Angus," Wiglaf said. "We will

never guess Seetha's weakness. I'm pinning my hopes on Aunt Lobelia."

Wiglaf and Angus hurried through dark hallways. At last they came to a wide door in the East Tower. Angus put the key in the lock. *Click!* The door opened.

Wiglaf stepped inside. It was very dark. He swallowed. Maybe breaking into a sorceress's room was not such a good idea. What if it was booby-trapped? What if Lobelia had cast spells against trespassers?

Angus felt his way over to the curtains. He pushed them back. Light flooded in.

Wiglaf looked around. He had expected to see shelves packed with jars of nettles and toadstools. He had very much hoped to see bottles labeled "Invisibility Potion" or "Dragon Repellent."

But instead he saw a fancy sitting room. Dozens of large trunks were lined up against the walls. In the far corner stood a three-sided mirror. Tapestries hung on the walls. Each one showed St. George in some bloody stage of killing a dragon. Wiglaf looked away. Even blood stitched into a tapestry made him sick.

"Maybe she keeps her potions in the trunks." Angus bent down to check one. "It's open," he whispered.

As Wiglaf helped him raise the lid, a husky voice called from the doorway: "Freeze!"

Wiglaf and Angus froze.

"Step away from the trunk," the voice went on. "And I mean *now*!"

Chapter 7

"Turn around, you little snoops," the voice said. "Let me have a look at you."

Wiglaf shook with fear as he turned.

"Aunt Lobelia!" Angus exclaimed.

"Angus?" The woman gasped. She dropped her traveling bags. "My stars!"

"I didn't know you were coming for a visit, Auntie," Angus said.

"That's pretty obvious," Lobelia told him.

Wiglaf saw that Angus's Aunt Lobelia had the same thick dark hair as Mordred. She had the same violet eyes, too. But the headmaster was stout. And Lobelia was as thin as a rail.

The sorceress did not look happy. Wiglaf swallowed. What if she turned him into a toad?

A pair of lean hounds with jeweled collars stood at Lobelia's side. The dogs began barking as they, too, recognized Angus.

"Shush, Demon! Lucifer, stop it!" Lobelia said. She threw off a blue velvet cape. Under it, she wore a silvery gown. "So, what are you two after? My jewels?"

"No, Auntie," Angus said. "I'm sorry we broke in. But it's an emergency. This is my friend Wiglaf. He needs help. The dragon Seetha is coming after him!"

"Seetha?" Lobelia cried. "The Beast from the East?"

Wiglaf nodded.

"So it's you she is after! But why?"

"Well, I...um, sort of...by accident, killed her son," Wiglaf explained.

"Bad move," Lobelia said. "On my way here, I passed through the village of Wormbelly. Seetha had just been there. And she left behind her horrible stink." Lobelia wrinkled her nose. "Someone should give that dragon a bottle of perfume. Anyway," she continued, "it seems that Seetha made a mistake. She thought the biggest, strongest man in Wormbelly killed her son. Oh, how she tortured the poor man! She made him play 'Ring Around the Rosie' until he fell down and could not get up."

"Say no more, I beg of you!" Wiglaf cried.

Lobelia shook her head. "Some villagers think he may get his wits back one day. But others fear the worst."

Wiglaf let out a little squeak.

"Seetha will be here at noon on Friday," Angus said. "Can you help Wiglaf, Auntie?"

"Of course I can help," Lobelia answered.

Wiglaf dropped to his knees. "Oh, thank you, Lady Lobelia!" Yes! A sorceress was going to use her magic to help him! Why, he was as good as saved. He grabbed Lobelia's hand and tried to kiss it.

Lobelia yanked her hand away. "Get up!" she ordered. Then she began circling Wiglaf.

She tilted her head. She looked at him from every which way.

"For starters," she said at last, "I'd lose the DSA tunic. And those old breeches. A leather tunic would be nice for you. Brown, to bring out the carrot color of your hair."

Wiglaf had never seen a sorceress at work before. But this was not what he had expected.

Lobelia walked over to her trunks. She started throwing open the lids. From one trunk, she pulled a shirt with billowing sleeves and a pair of quilted yellow breeches. From another, she took brown boots. From still another, forest green leggings and a helmet.

"The ram's horns on this helmet make a strong statement. Don't you think so?" Lobelia asked. "Oh! And this wolf pelt! It's perfect! You can drape it over one shoulder for a sort of Viking effect."

Lobelia piled the clothing into Wiglaf's arms. "Go behind that tapestry and change. We won't peek," she told him. "You know,

Wiglaf, clothes make the man. Or, in your case, the boy. Go on, now! Hurry!"

Wiglaf gave Angus a puzzled look. But he did as he was told. After all, who was he to question the ways of a sorceress?

Wiglaf took off his DSA tunic and his breeches. He put on the shirt. Then he pulled on the green leggings and the heavy yellow breeches. He slipped the leather tunic on over his head. He put on the tall boots and draped the wolf pelt over his shoulder, Viking style. Finally, he put the ram's-horn helmet on his head. He felt like a fool as he stepped out from behind the tapestry.

Demon and Lucifer began to growl at him.

Angus giggled—until a sharp look from Lobelia made him stop.

"Turn around, Wiglaf," Lobelia ordered. "Let me see the new you!"

Wiglaf turned.

"I am a genius!" Lobelia clapped her hands.

"Seetha will drop *dead* when she sees you!"

"She will?" Wiglaf exclaimed. "For sure?"

"Well, in a manner of speaking," Lobelia answered.

Wiglaf's heart sank. "I didn't think it could be that easy," he said. "But, Lady Lobelia! I need Seetha *really* and *truly* to drop dead! Or she will kill me! Oh, I know you have the power to help me! Angus said—" Wiglaf stopped. He shot a look at his friend.

"Said what?" Lobelia asked. She turned to her nephew. "Angus? Speak up!"

"I said..." Angus mumbled. "I said...uh...that you might be a sorceress."

"A sorceress!" Lobelia's eyes flashed with anger. "Who told you such a thing?"

"My mother," Angus answered.

"What? My own sister?" Lobelia cried.

Angus nodded. "She said that you could transform people. That you worked wonders."

"Oh, now I see." Lobelia smiled. "That part is true enough. I *do* transform people. Have you ever heard of King Richard the Lion-Hearted?"

Wiglaf and Angus nodded.

"Before I fixed him up, you know what people called him?" Lobelia asked. "Chicken-Hearted Richie, that's what! Who do you think put him in the bold red tunic? Who do you think told him to blacken his beard? Me!" Lobelia exclaimed. "Me!

"I transformed that man," she went on. "And I have transformed you, Wiglaf. Listen, if Seetha sees you as a little DSA student, she'll fry you! And from what I hear, she'll take her own sweet time about it, too."

Wiglaf swallowed.

"But," Lobelia went on, "if Seetha sees you as a mighty hero, she'll respect you. And who knows? Maybe she won't even kill you."

"That would be good," Wiglaf said. "Thank you, Lady Lobelia."

Lobelia smiled. "Dress like a hero, Wiglaf, and you *are* a hero. That's my motto!"

Chapter 8

"Sorry, Wiglaf," Angus said as he and Wiglaf left Lobelia's room.

"Me, too," Wiglaf said. He straightened his ram's-horn helmet. It was so heavy! And the wolf pelt made his neck itch. Worst of all, he didn't believe that the silly clothes would scare Seetha. He wished he had thought to get his clothes back from Lobelia. What would the other boys say when they saw him?

They reached Mordred's office. Angus opened the door and entered the room.

Wiglaf peeked in. He saw that Mordred had fallen asleep.

Angus reached up to put the key back.

But as he did, Mordred's eyes popped open.

"Angus?" he said. "What are you up to?" Then he saw Wiglaf at the door.

"Blazing King Ken's britches!" he yelled. He sat up. "What are *you* supposed to be?"

Wiglaf stepped into the headmaster's office.

"It's...er, a hero look, sir," he said.

"To scare off Seetha," Angus added.

"Bite your tongue, nephew!" Mordred exclaimed. "And never say the name of that no-good, no-gold dragon around me again!"

Mordred mopped his face with his big red hanky. He turned back to Wiglaf. "Where on earth did you ever get such a silly outfit?"

"Lady Lobelia gave me the clothes, sir," Wiglaf answered.

"Oh, Lobelia. That explains it." Mordred nodded. Then his eyes widened in horror. "Egad!" he cried. "Lobelia's *here*?"

"Yes, Uncle," Angus said.

"She never sent word that she was coming," Mordred complained. "I don't suppose she said how long she plans to stay."

Angus shook his head.

"Oh, I'm at death's door already! Five minutes with Lobelia will finish me off!" Mordred exclaimed. "Shoo, boys! Be off! Be gone! Leave me to enjoy what little peace I have left!"

Wiglaf backed away from the miserable headmaster. As he did, he saw a newspaper on Mordred's desk. The headline made Wiglaf's eyes widen in horror.

Wiglaf's hand shook as he picked up *The Medieval Times*. Angus looked over his shoulder. Together they read:

DRAGON LADY HUNTS SLAYER OF SON
Gorzil, Son #92, Was Mama's Darling Boy

RATSWHISKERS, Sept. 32nd
The dragon Seetha von Flambé, also known as the Beast from the East, is fighting mad. She and her late husband, Fangol, had some 3,684 young dragons. But one little dragon stood out from the others, and that was Gorzil.

"Gorzil was special," his mother told reporters just before she set fire to East Ratswhiskers yesterday. "When I find the brute who killed him, I don't know what I'll do. But it won't be pretty!"

Lifetime winner of the Stinkiest Dragon Award, Seetha is known as a fun-loving gal. She likes playing games. But when she plays games with her victims, Seetha has all the fun. She brought down Sir Featherbrain by making him do the hokeypokey until he could no longer put his left foot in. She has snuffed out the lives of other brave knights in ways too horrible to mention.

To the warrior who killed Seetha's darling boy, we can only say...Bye-bye!

Wiglaf gulped. He was more scared than he had ever been in his life. Now he almost wished Lobelia had turned him into a toad. At least he would be alive!

Chapter 9

Wiglaf didn't sleep a wink that night. On Thursday morning, he got up, thinking, *This could be the last day of my life!*

Well, he'd do his best to make it a good one.

Wiglaf put on his hero outfit and stuck his sword in his belt. He went to breakfast and ate some scrambled eel. Then he headed for Dragon Science Class with his friends.

"Ba— could be bats," Angus told Wiglaf as they walked. "Vampire bats are pretty scary."

"Maybe it's bandits," Erica put in.

"But Seetha has no gold for bandits to take," Angus said. "Hey! Maybe it's baked beans."

Wiglaf scratched his neck. The mangy wolf

pelt was giving him a nasty rash. He was hardly even listening to Angus and Erica who went on and on about every ba— word under the sun. He knew his friends were only trying to help. But what was the use? Guessing Seetha's secret weakness was impossible!

The three walked into science class.

"Looky! Looky!" Torblad yelled. "Here comes Mr. Puffy Pants!"

Wiglaf tried to look as if he didn't care. All day yesterday, boys had teased him. They said the wolf pelt looked like road kill. They said his helmet had cow horns on it. Every time he went by, they yelled out, *Moooo!* But Mr. Puffy Pants. That was even worse!

So much for having a good day.

"Button it up, Torblad!" Erica yelled back. "You *wish* you had puffy pants like Wiglaf's!"

The Dragon Science teacher, tall, thin Dr. Pluck, stood at the front of the room.

"**P**lease sto**p, pup**ils!" Dr. Pluck sputtered.

Dr. Pluck's lips were badly chapped because

he always spit when he said the letter *p*. DSA students made sure they came to Dr. Pluck's class early. They all wanted to get seats in the back rows to keep from getting sprayed.

Wiglaf, Erica, and Angus had not come early. So they took the only empty seats—in the first row.

"**P**lease **p**ay attention, **pup**ils," Dr. Pluck sputtered. He pulled down a large chart of a dragon. All its body parts were labeled. Dr. Pluck put his pointer on the dragon's belly. "The **plump p**art here is the **p**aunch," he told the class. "Its scientific name is the **pipp**i-hi**pp**o-**papp**a-**peep**us."

Erica's hand shot up. "Can you spell that for us, sir?"

"With **p**leasure," said Dr. Pluck. "**P**-i-**p**-**p**-"

Wiglaf didn't care about spelling right then. He didn't care about parts of a dragon. He didn't even care that Dr. Pluck was spraying him with spit. He stared at the dragon chart.

But all he could see was the face of Seetha from Brother Dave's book.

"The **pi**ppi-hi**pp**o-**papp**a-**pe**epus," Dr. Pluck went on, "is **p**acked with **p**artly digested **p**ieces of food. **P**ossibly **p**art of a **p**ossum. Or a **p**igeon. **P**lunge a s**p**ear into the dragon's **pi**ppi-hi**pp**o-**papp**a-**pe**epus—"

Dr. Pluck showered the class with facts. But Wiglaf was thinking of only one fact. Seetha was coming tomorrow!

Angus would never guess her secret weakness. Erica talked big. But talk was easy. She didn't stand a chance against the dragon. And Lobelia's hero outfit? What a joke! Seetha would see right through his clothes. And then she would know that, under the wolf pelt, he was anything but a hero.

Was there no one to help him?

"In a dragon's **pi**ppi-hi**pp**o-**papp**a-**pe**epus," Dr. Pluck was spraying, "might be a **p**ortion of a **p**ig or a—"

Wiglaf suddenly heard Dr. Pluck's words. Pig. Pig. PIG! Yes! Daisy might help him! True, she was a pig. But she was wiser than most people he knew. And, ever since the wizard Zelnoc had put a spell on her, Daisy could speak Pig Latin. Maybe she could tell him how to save himself. Even if she couldn't, Wiglaf wanted to see her. One last time.

So, after Dragon Science, Wiglaf cut Scrubbing. He headed for the henhouse.

"Daisy?" Wiglaf called softly. He didn't want to bother the hens. "Where are you?"

Wiglaf heard the patter of feet on the dirt floor. His pig dashed from her bed. She let out a scream.

Hens fluttered and squawked.

"It's me, Daisy!" Wiglaf exclaimed.

"Iglaf-way?" Daisy said, backing up.

"Of course it's me." Wiglaf took off the ram's-horn helmet. "See?"

Once Daisy and the hens got used to his

hero look, Wiglaf sat down with his pig. Daisy snuggled up to Wiglaf and listened as he told her about Gorzil's mother.

"Eetha-say?" Daisy gasped. "E-thay east-bay om-fray e-thay east-yay?"

"Yes. The Beast from the East." Wiglaf nodded sadly. "Her secret weakness begins with ba—. But that is all I know."

In a shaky voice Daisy said, "Acon-bay?"

"Maybe bacon *is* her weakness," Wiglaf said. "But I will never let Seetha get you, Daisy!" He planted a kiss on her snout. "The dragon will be here at noon tomorrow. What shall I do?"

"All-cay Elnoc-zay," the pig answered.

"The wizard?" Wiglaf said. "But Zelnoc's spells always turn out wrong. He said so himself. He was in for repairs when we met him."

"En-thay oo-whay?" Daisy asked.

"Who, indeed?" Wiglaf thought for a while. "All right, Daisy," he said at last. "I shall call Zelnoc. For even a broken wizard is better than no wizard at all."

Chapter 10

In those days, everyone knew how to call a wizard. All Wiglaf had to do was say Zelnoc's name backwards three times.

Wiglaf wrote on the dirt floor of the henhouse with his finger: Z E L N O C.

Then he wrote it backwards: C O N L E Z.

"Conlez, Conlez, Conlez," Wiglaf chanted.

Suddenly, a tiny bit of smoke appeared. It grew into a smoky, blue pillar. Out of the smoke stepped Zelnoc. He had on a pointed hat and a blue robe covered with stars.

"Bats and blisters!" Zelnoc yelled. "Am I called to a henhouse?" He turned to Wiglaf. "Who are you? Wait! Don't tell me. It's coming to me now. You tried to pull me out of Wizard's Bog. It's Wigwam, right?"

"Wiglaf, sir. Thank you for coming."

"You think I had a choice?" Zelnoc shook his head. "No such thing. When we wizards are called, we show up. Have to. It's Wizard Rule #598."

Now Daisy spoke. "Ello-hay, izard-way."

"Hello, pig! Where in the world did you learn to speak Pig Latin? Oh, I remember. My spell went wrong." Zelnoc sighed. "My spells always do. Well, what can I do for you, Wiglump? Tell me quickly! I want to get back to the Wizards' Convention. Zizmor the Amazing was just starting a demonstration. Oh, what that wizard can do with a few newts' eyes and a drop of bat's blood! And you should see his new wizard's staff. It's a ten-speed model! It casts any spell in half the time."

"I could use a fast spell," Wiglaf said. "For tomorrow, the dragon Seetha is coming to kill me."

"Seetha?" Zelnoc drew back from Wiglaf. "The Pest from the West?"

"No," said Wiglaf. "The Beast from the East."

"Humph," Zelnoc said. "Never heard of that one."

"Well, she's coming to get me," Wiglaf told the wizard. "I'm scared to death! That's why I called you. Can you cast a spell to help me?"

Zelnoc scratched his ear. "A courage spell would fix you up. But can I remember one?"

Zelnoc thought for a minute. Then he snapped his fingers. "Got it! Quick, Wigloaf! Let me say it over you before I forget."

Zelnoc pushed up his sleeves. He stretched out his arms toward Wiglaf. He waggled his fingers.

"Just loosening myself up a bit," the wizard said. "All right. Count to three for me, pig."

"One-yay," said Daisy. "Oo-tway. Ee-thray!"

Zelnoc began to chant:

"Roses are red.

Violets are blue.

Sugar is—"

"Excuse me, sir?" Wiglaf broke in.

"Never stop a wizard midspell!" Zelnoc yelled. "Never!"

"But are you sure that's how a *courage* spell starts?" Wiglaf asked.

Zelnoc thought for a moment. "It doesn't sound right, does it?" He tapped his head with his finger. "Oh, courage spell? Where are you? Ah! There you are! Count again, pig!"

Daisy did: "One-yay. Oo-tway. Ee-thray!"

Zelnoc put one hand on his hip. He bent his other arm and stuck it out to the side. Then he began to sing:

"I'm a little teapot, short and stout!

Here is my handle! Here is my spout!"

"Op-stay, izard-way!" Daisy yelled.

"Sir!" Wiglaf cried. "That can not be it either!"

"Oh, toads and warts!" Zelnoc exclaimed. "I'll call Zizmor. He'll get it right."

Zelnoc shut his eyes and chanted: "*Romziz, Romziz, Romziz!*"

Nothing happened.

He tried again. "*Romziz, Romziz, Romziz!*"

Again, nothing happened.

"Slugs and leeches!" Zelnoc roared. He threw his pointed hat to the ground. He began jumping up and down on it, shouting over and over, "*Romziz! Romziz! Romziz!*"

POOF! Smoke filled the henhouse. Red smoke. Yellow smoke. Bright purple smoke.

The hens sprang from their nests. They raced out of the henhouse, clucking loudly.

"Un-ray, Iglaf-way!" Daisy yelled.

But Wiglaf stood where he was. He watched in amazement as the smoke swirled into great columns. Out of each column stepped a wizard wearing a gown the color of the smoke. Some two dozen wizards appeared in all. They looked around, muttering.

"Zelnoc?" Wiglaf whispered. "Are these friends of yours?"

"Oh, my stars!" Zelnoc exclaimed. "I've called the whole convention!"

A very tall red-robed wizard with bright red eyes pounded his staff on the floor. The other wizards quieted.

"Did you call me?" the red wizard asked Wiglaf.

"Why...no, sir," Wiglaf said. "You see, Zelnoc thought—"

"Zelnoc!" The red wizard whirled around. "You! I should have known!"

"Sorry, Amazing One," Zelnoc said. He picked up his crumpled hat and stuck it on his head. "I only meant to call you, Ziz. Just you."

Zizmor the Amazing snorted. "Well, what did you want?"

"Tomorrow, this poor boy must fight Seetha," Zelnoc said. He pushed Wiglaf forward.

"Seetha?" Zizmor gasped. "The Beast from the East?"

"Yes, sir," Wiglaf answered.

The lesser wizards whispered darkly among themselves: "Oh, he's a goner. Poor boy. Doesn't stand a chance."

"So," Zelnoc continued, "I said to myself, 'Zelnoc, old sock, old bean, who better to cast a courage spell on this poor lad than Zizmor the Amazing?'"

Zizmor raised an eyebrow. "As it happens, I have been working on a new courage spell. But it's still in the experimental stage."

"I'll try anything!" Wiglaf said. "Please, sir! Can you help me?"

"Does a troll live under a bridge?" Zizmor answered. "Of course I can. And I shall. With pleasure. I would dearly love to take revenge on that fire-breathing beast myself."

"Why is that, sir?" Wiglaf asked.

"Seetha burned down my tower," Zizmor

said. "For no reason. Just flew over, leaned down, and torched it." The Amazing One shook his head. "It's been nothing but carpenters, painters, plumbers, and stonemasons ever since. I hate to think what the final bill is going to be." He closed his red eyes. He breathed deeply to calm himself.

"All right, my boy," Zizmor said, opening his eyes once more. "Are you ready for a dose of courage?"

"I think so, sir," Wiglaf answered.

"I shall give you a double dose," Zizmor said. "No, for Seetha, triple, I think. My triple spell doesn't last too long. But while it's working it's a zinger!"

"Ood-gay uck-lay iglaf-Way!" Daisy whispered.

Wiglaf waved to his pig. Then he crossed his fingers for luck and got ready for the spell.

Zizmor the Amazing called his fellow wizards to make a circle around Wiglaf. They all stretched out their arms toward him. Zizmor held his ten-speed staff over Wiglaf's head. In a low voice, he chanted:

"Spineless, gutless, weak-kneed brat,
Chicken-hearted scaredy-cat,
Cringing coward, yellow-belly,
Lily-livered, heart of jelly.
Change this boy who's standing here,
Into He-Who-Knows-No-Fear!"

Sparks began to fly from Zizmor's staff.

Wiglaf gasped as they showered down on him. *Ziz! Ziz! Ziz!* The sparks flashed and popped. The roar of rushing wind filled Wiglaf's ears. And then the wizards began to swirl before his eyes.

The next thing Wiglaf knew, he was lying on the henhouse floor.

All the wizards stared down at him.

Zelnoc's face appeared close to Wiglaf's. "Speak to me, lad!" he cried. "Speak to me!"

Chapter 11

"Where is Seetha?" Wiglaf growled. He leaped to his feet. "Where is that ugly dragon?"

"Uh—thought you said she was coming tomorrow," Zelnoc said.

"I can't wait until tomorrow!" Wiglaf exclaimed.

He snatched his ram's-horn helmet from the floor. He jammed it on his head. "I shall save the world from the Beast from the East today! First, I shall slash Seetha's throat!" He drew his sword and sliced at the air. "Then I shall stab her through the heart!" He lunged forward, shouting, "Take *that*, you scaly scavenger!"

"Oh, dear," Zelnoc said. "Maybe the triple spell was a little much, Ziz."

"Fiddlesticks," Zizmor scoffed. "All right, fellow enchanters!" he called to the other wizards. "Clearly our work here is finished. Let's get back to the convention, shall we? I believe there's a brew-tasting party tonight."

"Wait for me, Ziz!" Zelnoc said. "Good luck, Wigloop!"

"Luck? Who needs luck?" Wiglaf exclaimed. "Not I! For I have courage!"

"Oh, dear," Zelnoc said again as smoke began to fill the henhouse.

Ten seconds later, both the smoke and the wizards had disappeared.

Wiglaf charged out of the henhouse. He waved his sword and shouted:

"Look out, Seetha! Here I come!
DSA ! That's where I'm from!
Will I slay you?
Yes! I will!
Here I come to kill! Kill! Kill!"

Daisy ran to the henhouse door. She called after him, "Ait-way, Iglaf-way!"

"Sorry, pork chop," Wiglaf called back. "I have a dragon to slay!"

He-Who-Knows-No-Fear marched across the castle yard. From the tips of the ram's horns on his helmet down to the toes of his new boots, every inch of him was filled with courage. There was only one thing he wanted—action!

"Seetha's a fun-loving dragon, is she?" Wiglaf growled. "Well! Let's see how much fun she has when I stab her in the pippi-hippo-pappa-peepus!"

Wiglaf saw that Sir Mort had brought the Class I students out to the castle steps. They were having a Rubbish Relay. This was a scheme of Mordred's for getting the litter in the castle yard picked up.

"Wiglaf!" Erica called. "We were looking for you!" She and Angus broke away from the group. They ran up to him.

Angus waved a piece of parchment. "I've started a ba— list. I'll find Seetha's weakness yet! Listen—bald men, ballet dancers, bank robbers, barbers, baton twirlers, barking dogs—"

"Stop!" Wiglaf yelled. "What care I for Seetha's weakness? I shall slay her with my sword!"

Erica's eyes grew wide. "Wiglaf! You don't sound like yourself. Where are you going, anyway?"

"I am off to find the Beast from the East!" Wiglaf exclaimed. "I'll not wait for her to hunt me down. Nay! I shall hunt *her* down! I shall cut that dragon into a thousand pieces!"

"All *right*, Wiggie!" Erica punched her fist in the air. "You speak like a true dragon slayer at last!"

Wiglaf squared his shoulders. He marched through the gatehouse. He started across the drawbridge. Erica and Angus had to run to keep up with him.

"Look!" Angus yelled. He stopped suddenly. "Some strange creature is coming!"

"Creature?" Wiglaf drew his sword. "Never fear! I shall protect you!"

He looked where Angus was pointing. A giant rabbit was hopping toward the drawbridge.

"Run!" the rabbit screamed as it hopped. "Run for your lives!"

Wiglaf stuck his sword back in his belt. It would not do to slay such a helpless creature.

"You heard the rabbit!" Angus cried. "Quick! Into the castle!" He grabbed Wiglaf by the wolf pelt. He tried to drag him back toward the gatehouse.

"Unhand me, man!" Wiglaf cried. He struggled with Angus.

The rabbit hopped closer. Wiglaf saw that it wasn't a rabbit at all. It was a man in a bunny suit.

Erica eyed the rabbit. "Yorick?" she said. "Is that you?"

"It's me," the rabbit said. "I have come to say I was wrong. Seetha won't be here at noon on

Friday. You see, I should have multiplied the wind speed by the width of the smoke cloud. Then divided—"

"Out with it, Yorick!" Wiglaf roared.

"Seetha will be here at noon on *Thursday*," Yorick told them.

"But today is Thursday!" Angus pointed out. "And it's almost noon!"

"Right," Yorick said. "And guess what? Seetha is here!"

Chapter 12

Wiglaf raised his eyes to the sky. Far away, he saw a small, dark cloud. He sniffed the air. Pew! It smelled like rotten eggs.

Wiglaf centered his ram's-horn helmet. He brushed off his wolf pelt. He drew his sword. Then he struck a manly pose on the drawbridge.

"Seetha, you have but little time to live!" Wiglaf roared at the sky. "For I was born to slay you!"

Yorick backed slowly away from Wiglaf. Then he turned and ran across the drawbridge as fast as the legs of his bunny suit would allow. "She's here!" he yelled. "Seetha's here!"

Mordred stuck his head out a tower window. "Seetha's here?" he cried. "Egad!"

"Seetha comes to meet her doom!" Wiglaf called up to the headmaster. "That's me," he added. "*I* am her doom!"

"Oh, right." Mordred rolled his violet eyes. Then he stuck a whistle in his mouth. He blew it until his face was as red as his pajamas, which he still had on.

"Everybody into the castle!" he called. "Hurry now! Step on it, Angus! You, too, Eric!"

"No!" Erica called back. "I shall stay and fight the dragon!"

"Me, too, I guess," said Angus.

Wiglaf looked up. The dark cloud was blowing quickly toward DSA.

"Angus!" Mordred yelled. "Get inside! Do you know what your mother would do to me if I let a dragon get you?"

"Sorry, Wiglaf." Angus shrugged. Then he ran into the castle with surprising speed.

The dark cloud began to drop. Wiglaf saw green smoke puff out from its edges. But its middle was as dark as midnight.

"You, too, Eric!" Mordred yelled. "Inside!"

"No, sir!" Erica cried. "I must fight beside Wiglaf!"

The cloud dropped lower. The smell of rotten eggs grew stronger.

"Into the castle!" Mordred roared. "Now!"

Thunder rumbled from inside the cloud.

"Never!" Erica cried. "I shall not leave my friend in battle! That's Dragon Slayers' Rule #37!"

Once more Mordred's face began to turn as red as his pajamas.

"I *order* you into the castle!" he yelled. "Get in here now! Or turn in the Dragon Slayer of the Month Medal."

Erica gasped. She clutched at her medal.

"Do as he says!" Wiglaf told her. "Seetha is my dragon! This is my fight!"

Erica looked from Wiglaf to Mordred and

back to Wiglaf. "Oh, all right," she said at last. "But take this." She put a small, pointy dagger into Wiglaf's hand. "It's from *The Sir Lancelot Catalog*. It's called Stinger. Good luck, Wiggie!"

So saying, Erica walked sadly across the drawbridge. Wiglaf stuck the dagger into his boot. He stood alone outside the castle. The smoky, smelly, rumbling cloud stopped right over DSA.

"I'm waiting for you, Seetha!" Wiglaf yelled.

The cloud began to drop. Then out of the smoke poked the ugly head of Seetha. Her yellow eyes glowed. Her long tongue flicked out of her mouth. "WAIT NO MORE!" she cried.

Wiglaf gagged as the dragon's breath hit him. It smelled like a garbage dump come to life.

Seetha spread her wings. She flew down from her cloud. She landed beside the moat.

Her smell landed with her. Wiglaf almost

wished Zizmor had changed him into He-Who-Smells-No-Foul-Odors. Seetha was one stinky dragon!

"I AM SEETHA!" the dragon roared. "WHOEVER KILLED MY DARLING BOY—PREPARE TO DIE!"

Chapter 13

"I killed Gorzil!" He-Who-Knows-No-Fear shouted to the dragon.

"YOU?" Seetha drew her lips back from her pointy teeth in what Wiglaf guessed was a smile. "YOU ARE NOT BIG ENOUGH TO KILL A FLEA!"

"I did the deed," Wiglaf yelled. "Me! Wiglaf of Pinwick, Dragon Slayer!"

"THEN TELL ME, WIGLAF, HOW DID GORZIL DIE? LAUGHING AT YOUR SILLY CLOTHES?"

"He died laughing," Wiglaf answered. "Laughing at some jokes I told him. Bad jokes. *Really* bad."

"OH!" Seetha gasped. "YOU GUESSED

HIS SECRET WEAKNESS!" Large orange tears oozed out of her eyes. They rolled down her scaly cheeks. She sniffed. "MY GORZIE WAS EVERYTHING A YOUNG DRAGON SHOULD BE!" she cried. "THE DARLING BOY WAS GREEDY! LAZY! RUDE! CRUEL! HE CHEATED EVERY CHANCE HE GOT! HE WAS...PERFECT!"

Seetha swiped a claw across her runny nose. "BUT ENOUGH CHIT-CHAT!" she roared. "IT'S PAYBACK TIME!"

Seetha flew up and landed on the castle wall. She looked around. Her eyes found Coach Plungett's practice dragon in the castle yard.

"LET ME GIVE YOU A LITTLE DEMON-STRATION! HERE'S A GAME YOU AND I MIGHT PLAY, WIGLAF!" Seetha exclaimed. "SPIT BALL!"

She made a hacking sound in the back of her throat. Up came a blob of fire. She spit it at the straw dragon. WHOOSH! It burst into flames.

Mordred poked his head out of the tower

window. He cupped his hands to his mouth.

"Excuse me, dragon lady, ma'am?" he called.

Seetha turned toward the window. "AND YOU WOULD BE..."

"Mordred, Your Scaliness. I'm Headmaster of Dragon Sla...um, of this school." He bowed. "Go ahead and have your fun with the boy. But, please. Try not to set the school on fire. I'm afraid that if a spark hits the—"

Seetha cut him off by spitting a fire ball at his head. The headmaster quickly disappeared from the window.

Seetha flew back down to the grass near Wiglaf. "NOW...HOW SHALL I DO YOU IN?" She tapped a claw on her scales, thinking. "WE COULD PLAY BADMINTON—WITH YOU AS THE BIRDIE."

"Whatever, Seetha!" Wiglaf growled. "But I swear by the ram's horns on my helmet that *you* shall be the one to die!" He waved his sword in the air. And with a mighty battle cry he charged at the beast.

Seetha's eyes widened with surprise. Then she blew a puff of red-hot dragon breath right at Wiglaf.

The blast of smelly heat almost knocked Wiglaf off his feet. His wolf pelt crackled. It curled at the edges. Sweat popped out on his brow. But still he ran towards the dragon.

With one claw, Seetha knocked the sword out of Wiglaf's hand. With the other, she struck him. He went rolling head over heels.

Wiglaf came to a stop near the edge of the moat. Before he could get back on his feet, Seetha struck again. She hooked Wiglaf's wolf pelt with her claw. She lifted him up off the ground.

Wiglaf swayed crazily in the air as the dragon lifted him higher and higher. Soon he was face to face with Gorzil's awful mother.

"Back off, smelly one!" Wiglaf cried. "A thousands skunks are not as stinky as you."

Seetha smiled. "Thank you," she said.

Wiglaf was only inches from Seetha's face.

He saw that her scales were covered with dirt and scum. A crust of old, dried slime coated her nose. Her moss-covered fangs had holes in them the size of dinner plates.

"HMMMM...WHAT'S THE *WORST* WAY FOR YOU TO DIE?" Seetha said. "I KNOW! THE TICKLE TORTURE! YOU'LL DIE LAUGHING—JUST LIKE MY GORZIE!"

"Not me!" cried He-Who-Knows-No-Fear. "I can take it!" The dragon's dirty claw came closer and closer to him.

"KITCHY-KITCHY-KOO!" Seetha cried. She tickled Wiglaf's tummy. His neck. His armpits. "KITCHY-KITCHY-KOO!"

But Wiglaf never even smiled.

"NO FAIR! YOU'RE NOT TICKLISH!" Seetha pouted for a minute. "BUT I KNOW MORE GAMES. MANY MORE! LET'S PLAY 'HIGH DIVE'!"

Still clutching Wiglaf, Seetha spread her wings and took off. She landed on the gatehouse roof. She held Wiglaf out, over the moat. "CAN YOU DO A JACKKNIFE WITH A HALF TWIST? HMMMMM?"

Wiglaf looked down. Hundreds of eels looked up at him. They hungrily snapped their jaws.

"You can't scare me, Seetha!" Wiglaf yelled. He drew Erica's dagger from his boot. "For I am He-Who-Knows-No-Fear!"

"OH, YEAH?" the dragon roared. "WELL, I AM SHE-WHO-MAKES-BRAVE-KNIGHTS-CRY-LIKE-BABIES!"

Wiglaf opened his mouth to reply. But a dizzy feeling swept over him. Bright lights flashed. He heard the rush of wind. Seetha's face seemed to melt.

He squeezed his eyes shut.

When he opened them again, the courage spell was broken.

He-Who-Knows-No-Fear was gone.

Now, caught in the dragon's claw was plain old Chicken-Hearted Wiglaf.

Chapter 14

"Ayiiiiiiiiiiiiiiiiiiiiiiiii!" screamed Wiglaf. His heart thumped with terror. Any second, Seetha would roast him! Or toast him! Or feed him to the eels!

He tried covering his eyes with his hands. But...what was *this* in his hand?

"MAYBE YOU SHOULD TRY A DOUBLE SOMERSAULT!" Seetha roared. She dangled Wiglaf further out over the moat.

Wiglaf didn't answer. He stared at the dagger. What a sharp, sharp point it had. He could stab Seetha with it. But the very thought made him feel sick. With a shudder, Wiglaf let the dagger slip from his hand.

"*OW!*" Seetha yelped as Stinger stuck her. "MY TOE! MY BEAUTIFUL BIG TOE! WHAT HAVE YOU DONE?"

Seetha tossed Wiglaf away. He sailed through the air. With a thump, he landed on the ground. He bounced twice. Then he lay still.

Above him, the dragon howled in pain. "MY FAVORITE TOE! IT'S BLEEDING!"

Wiglaf moaned. He would be bruised all over. But thanks to Lobelia's heavy leather tunic and thick, quilted breeches, he would live. He pulled himself slowly to his feet.

The dragon rocked back and forth on the gatehouse roof. "LET ME KISS YOU AND MAKE YOU ALL BETTER!" she said to her toe.

Wiglaf glanced up. Seetha held her hurt foot in her front claws. She puckered up her purple lips. With a loud SMACK! she planted a kiss on her toe.

Then Seetha began hopping up and down on her good foot. "I'LL GET YOU, WIGLAF!" she roared. "I'LL MAKE YOU SIZZLE LIKE A FRENCH FRY!"

Wiglaf groaned.

He was a goner!

So Wiglaf did what any chicken-hearted boy would do. He crouched down. He covered his eyes and shook with fear.

"HERE I COME!" Seetha screamed. "I'LL...WHOA! HEY! WHOOO!"

Wiglaf peeked out from behind his fingers.

Seetha teetered on the roof above him. She still held her hurt toe. But something was wrong. Her wings flapped clumsily. Her tail lashed the air. She swayed dangerously back and forth. She lost her balance. Down she plunged.

SPLASH!

Seetha hit the moat.

A huge cloud of steam rose from the waters.

Wiglaf couldn't see a thing.

Suddenly, the dragon lurched up, out of the mist.

Wiglaf jumped back.

"HELP!" Seetha screamed. "HELP ME, YOU FOOLISH BOY!"

But Wiglaf was not *that* foolish.

Seetha kicked and splashed. She slapped the water with her tail.

Wiglaf saw that Seetha's scales looked clean but dull. Her yellow eyes had faded, too. Her horn was drooping to one side. Her tongue hung out the side of her mouth.

"I CAN'T TAKE THIS MUCH LONGER!" Seetha cried. "HELP ME! I'LL GIVE YOU HEAPS OF GOLD!"

Before Wiglaf could shake his head *no*, Mordred leaned out the castle window. "Gold?" he called. "But everyone knows that you have no gold, Seetha!"

"HA!" Seetha laughed. "THAT OLD RUMOR? I'VE GOT MORE GOLD THAN

ANY TEN DRAGONS PUT TOGETHER!
AND I HID IT ALL IN THE DARK
FOOOOLUB—"

She disappeared under the water again.

Suddenly the drawbridge came down with a bang.

Mordred zoomed out of the castle. He pushed Wiglaf out of the way. He dropped to his knees.

"Seetha!" he cried. "Madam Seetha! Can you hear me?"

"GLUG-GOLD!" Seetha sputtered, popping up. "GET ME OUT OF HERE, BIG BOY— AND IT'S YOURS!"

"Mine?" Mordred gasped as Seetha sank. "Come back, Madam! We have to talk!"

Only Seetha's purple lips popped up now. "GOLBLUB....GLOOOOPH!" The dragon belched and disappeared.

"Hold on, Seetha!" Mordred cried. "I'll save you!" And the headmaster of Dragon Slayers'

Academy dove into the moat to rescue the dragon.

Wiglaf stood alone on the drawbridge. He watched Mordred dive down to find the dragon.

But it was no use.

Seetha's head never again appeared above the dark and murky waters of the moat.

But Mordred's did. "Dragons don't drown!" he cried at last. "How can this be happening?"

Suddenly Wiglaf knew the answer.

"Seetha died from her secret weakness!" he called to the soggy headmaster. "It was a *bath* that killed the beast!"

Wiglaf straightened his ram's-horn helmet.

Then, with his head held high, he walked across the drawbridge and back to DSA.

Mordred stood before all the DSA students in the dining hall that night.

"Did Wiglaf ask Seetha about her gold?" he asked in a hoarse voice.

"Nooooo!" Mordred answered himself. "So I have none of it! Not a single gold coin! All I have—" he sneezed loudly into his red hanky "—is double pneumonia!"

Mordred covered his face with his hands. He began to cry.

"I have some bad news, too," Frypot told the students. The cook made his way to the front of the room.

"When Seetha fell into the moat," he continued, "that filthy dragon poisoned the eels! She killed every single one of them dead."

"What?" Mordred lifted his tear-stained face. "You mean now I have to *buy* groceries to feed all these little gluttons? Oh, this *is* cruel!"

"I'm sorry to tell you this, boys," Frypot went on. "But your days of eating my yummy eel dishes are over."

A hush fell over the great hall.

Then all the students jumped to their feet. They began clapping and stomping and whistling.

Angus shot Wiglaf a thumbs-up sign. "Let's give a cheer for Wiglaf!" he cried.

And they all began to shout. Even Erica, the only DSA student who would actually miss Frypot's eels:

> *"No more eel! No more eel!*
> *Never again for any meal!*
> *Wiglaf! Wiglaf! He's our man!*
> *If he can do it, anybody can!*
> *Yeaaaaaaaaaa Wiglaf!"*

The students kept clapping and cheering. It warmed Wiglaf's heart. Maybe he hadn't killed Seetha with his sword. Maybe his courage had come from a wizard's spell. But tonight in the DSA dining hall, he was certainly a hero.

**Find out what new adventures
await our hero in:**

Dragon Slayers' Academy ™ 3

Class Trip To
The Cave of Doom

Poor Wiglaf! He has slain two dragons, Gorzil and his mother Seetha von Flambé, but he has no gold to show for it. Now Mordred, the money-hungry headmaster of Dragon Slayers' Academy, is sending everyone on a class trip to find Seetha's gold.

So everyone sets off on a medieval campout—there's ghost stories, an angry troll, a mad hermit, booby traps galore, and a surprise visitor who really shakes things up.